Stagnant Water

A Novel

Gaeli Love Weiss

ISBN: 979-8-218-27326-2

Dedicated to
Danny and Mara.
And the Weiss family for
100 years of loving the Ozarks.

Summer

Chapter One

My father is dead 'n I shouldn't feel like this anymore, Naomi thinks, only moments after entering the historic church where his funeral is in progress. It's the first time she's seen him in years. It's the first time she's been to church in years, too.

Whenever her mind flickers to the old place, Naomi pictures it dirty and rotted. The roof mossy with missing shingles. Birds nesting in the gutters and their white shit splattered all over the steps. The stained glass she spent so many mornings and a good few nights staring up at, shattered. The colorful pieces laying on the pews.

But here she sits. The wood beneath her, and that stained-glass window looking down on her. Blaire Baptist Church stands pearly and tall in between the dusty summer homes of the rich folk of Kansas City and St. Louis, and the trailer homes of those that have planted themselves in the Ozark soil long ago.

Naomi has despised the entire affair for as long as she can remember. When she was small, she dreamed of playing hooky on Sunday mornings and Wednesday evenings. Anything to escape the dresses and tights and those squeaky black Mary Janes her mama would force her into. She supposes that few children enjoy sitting for service. It's natural to be antsy when those wide, tall windows frame a sea of hickory trees to be climbed.

They oughta just board these up 'n not torture us anymore. Why the hell would you be inside on a day like this?

Beyond the dome of emerald leaves are heaving rolls of clouds. After months of sunshine and scorching heat, a few dreary days are more than welcome. The rain does everyone some good.

Small droplets begin to appear on the windows beside Naomi's pew. They race to the bottom of the pane and merge with one another before dropping to the dirt and rock below. Naomi's eyes follow one after another.

"Please rise." A wave of black shoulders ascend from the pews and Naomi reluctantly follows suit.

The big pine box sits at the front surrounded by roses — bouquets of white and green and red. Beside it, a framed photo of the man within is centered in a floral wreath with a brass plaque reading:

"In loving memory of
Marshal and Reverend Edward David Darby
1967 — 2021"

In the picture, he wears a black suit with a starched white button-up and a red tie. His goatee and eyebrows are dark and bushy, and his head is as bald as she remembered.

It looks like it was taken around the time she last saw him. Naomi wonders if his hair had begun to gray since then. Or if his skin had wrinkled more or his teeth had yellowed.

I hope it'll rain on the big bastard when they take him outside. Maybe it'll wash him down the river 'n his bloated, ugly corpse'll get ate by catfish and he'll never get to be buried 'n he'll never even get to Hell.

But then, she counters herself, *he wouldn't get an eternity of torture in Hell if he sunk to the bottom of the river. But I suppose this is all bullshit anyhow. Maybe his body gettin' ate by catfish while his "soul" disappears 'n with it goes his hope of God 'n heaven 'n eternal salvation. It all oughta get thrown to the fish.*

The prayer begins, and Naomi takes the chance to spy on those seated around her. She tried to get there as late as possible to avoid any unwanted interactions — and all interactions here are unwanted. She tucked herself away in one of the back rows with a few elderly folks and mothers with small babies that were sure to cry at least once during the ceremony.

Across the aisle are the butcher and his wife, Mrs. Redfield, the second-grade teacher in Blaire. Their youngest son, who must be close to the second grade himself, gazes down respectfully alongside his parents. Years ago, Mrs. Redfield was Naomi's teacher. Naomi remembers her being harsh for elementary school. Corporal punishment wasn't uncommon here.

The worst of that for Naomi had been on a hot day at the beginning of her second-grade year. All the kids were out playing during recess despite the pavement being sweltering enough to burn. Naomi and a few other children had been hiding behind the equipment shed. One of the other girls — Naomi has long since forgotten who, but she recalls that the girl was a few years older — had pulled her shirt up and let the others touch her new, jealousy-inducing B-cups. Mrs. Redfield caught Naomi with a tiny, grimy hand on the girl's breast, which was mortifying enough on its own.

"Did anyone else touch her?" Mrs. Redfield stood above three or four elementary-aged girls who were hot-faced and ready to never speak of this again. They all said no. "You're dismissed."

Naomi couldn't move. She knew Mrs. Redfield didn't mean her and that there was hell to pay. Her eyes had already become misty, making it difficult to read the teacher's facial expression. So, she kept her head down. It was well over ninety degrees out, but it was the embarrassment that felt hot enough to melt her.

I won't never do it again. I won't never do it again. Dear God, if you let me go I won't never do it again. I swear. Naomi repeated to herself in the hope that God would restart the whole day and this incident would have never happened and she could live her life without Mrs. Redfield keeping her there out of all the girls. *Oh God, she's gonna tell Father.* Naomi's heart dropped and she knew her pleading with God was hopeless. He always sided with her father.

"Little girls often find themselves interested in a woman's figure. In a few years, it'll be your figure too. Little girls make the mistake of gettin' ahead of themselves though. You'll be a woman soon enough and then you won't have to molest the others. You know that what you did was wrong?"

Naomi nodded her head yes but kept her eyes down so her tears could fall to the asphalt and sizzle away, unseen.

Mrs. Redfield squatted down in front of the girl to prevent that blessing of privacy.

"Your father must've taught you 'bout the sins by now. Do you know lust? Now I know that's not what was happenin' here. But it's an awful thin line and it's best that we do what we can to stop that temptation."

Naomi felt sweat slip between her shoulder blades and down the backs of her thighs. She felt like a slug. She touched something forbidden and so she was going to be salted and shrivel to nothing.

Mrs. Redfield held out her hand to the child and Naomi handed herself over. "We're gonna give you a taste of the hellfire that'll lick you if you let this incident become somethin' more than a child's curiosity." Then the woman turned Naomi's palm down to the asphalt and laid it there like a sausage on a skillet.

The sound of benches creaking pulls Naomi from her memories. The crowd stands and the pallbearers approach the unstained casket — her younger brother, Aaron, among them. His hair is still the same dark curls their father had when he was their age. It's been years since she saw him. His black suit matches the one in their father's memorial photo.

The men hoist the oversized casket to their shoulders with beads of sweat pooling on their brows and darkening the cloth at their necks. It's a terribly hot day to be crammed inside the historic church. It's a terribly hot day to be shoved into a wooden box and buried in the cool, damp earth.

It's too generous for the ol' fucker, Naomi seethes. *He deserves an end hotter than this.*

As they march down the middle aisle, taking with them Blaire's sole preacher and town marshal, the slips of skin by Naomi's fingernails start to sting from picking at them. She thinks of all of the times she wished law enforcement were the way they are in the old Westerns her father allowed her to watch: men full of valor and fighting against all odds to do the right thing. She also watched them with her mama's mama, Grandma Dottie, where the folks in uniform cared about the little guy and got into silly mishaps.

An actual pig's got more respect than Father, Naomi thinks.

Everyone begins to congregate at the front doors and in between aisles, taking their cue to leave for supper at the Darby family home. It's tradition to eat until bursting after the loss of a community member. Naomi remains seated, despite how much she misses her paternal grandmother's cooking. Growing up, her mama copied Grandma Joyce's recipes but they were lukewarm imitations at best. Grandma Joyce's suppers always fogged up Aaron's glasses and the aroma would fill the room from ceiling to floor. The kind of scent that made you hungry on a full stomach.

"I'm so happy you came," a soft lilting voice comes from behind Naomi. She turns from watching through the windows as the pallbearers carry the casket over the well-worn path to reach the graveyard. The dead man is slowly swallowed whole by the reaching branches of the woods.

Grandma Joyce is a small woman. Her hair is kept up in pins in the heavy, humid climate. She waves a small paper fan by her face, fluttering the wisps of hair that escaped. "They'll be back soon. Your brother'd like to see you. I shouldn't be sayin' nothin', but he and his wife are tryin'. Ain't that somethin'?" A glimmer of hope in her grief.

"That's good." Naomi doesn't match her grandma's lightness, although she tries.

Aaron's three years younger than Naomi. From the time he was born, Eddie groomed him to be the next leader of Blaire Baptist. It was essential that Aaron felt the glory of the wrath of God from an early age. That he was emboldened to have a direct line of communication with the Lord. Their father had high demands of his children and often cruel methods for ensuring orders were followed. However, those methods differed between the children. Black eyes and swollen wrists were not fitting for the future Reverend Darby, after all.

When Aaron would skip Sunday school or misremember Bible verses, he was locked in the root cellar behind the house. Naomi did receive this punishment as well, but it didn't matter if God came to her while she was in the dark.

"You get a dog yet? I told you the Sinclair's had a litter 'bout seven weeks ago. Their pointer got out and met some mutt. Theresa's awful upset about it. There's a lotta folks that woulda paid a penny for some purebred huntin' dogs but that ain't what you need it for. Might as well call 'em," Grandma Joyce continues.

"Maybe," replies Naomi half-heartedly. Her father never allowed the family to have one, citing them as being dirty and stupid and needing more food than they could provide. In truth, Naomi is consumed by guilt for even considering the idea. She doesn't know how to care for another — even a dog. Not to mention with her father dead and gone, and her mama and brother free from him, it's finally Naomi's time to leave. She doesn't need to bring any living being besides herself out of this town. "I guess I oughta say hello to Mama and Aaron," Naomi begins to step aside when her grandma places a wrinkled hand upon her arm.

"I don't presume to know how you're feelin' in all of this. Do try to let your anger leave your heart though. It can weigh so heavy it'll pull you to Hell without you needin' to do nothin' else," her eyes pierce Naomi's, and she is filled with that old familiar swell of guilt that she's come to realize only family can inspire.

So you don't even need to sin to get there. We're all fucked, Naomi thinks.

"I'm alright, Grandma. Maybe I'll see you for supper." With no intention of keeping that pseudo-promise, the young woman side-steps into the aisle.

The black and orange dress her grandma wears clings to the sweat on her legs, and she readjusts herself before exiting. Naomi follows behind and kisses the top of the elderly woman's head.

Chapter Two

The assortment of old cars and trucks has dissipated to only a handful. Naomi sees her father's ancient gray sedan. He purchased it in '98 and did all the maintenance on it himself. She vaguely considers who will work on it now, but notices that her mama sits by herself in the cab, eyes locked on the barrier of woods her husband had been escorted through.

Naomi watches her for only a few moments before Margaret turns toward her. An unsure hand raises an awkward greeting to her mama. But Margaret's dark eyes quickly look back in the direction where Eddie's body is being locked away from them forever.

This reaction should have been expected. Although neither Naomi nor Aaron had known the extent to which Eddie hurt her, they knew he did not spare the literal or metaphoric rod for anyone in the family. There was never any solidarity in the Darby home.

Naomi once hoped for it with all her heart, with her every prayer to an absent God. She would beg the Lord to tell her brother to hold her hand at night now and again. A small gift that she extended to Aaron whenever Father would punish him. She begged that God would change His mind and that kneeling on the unforgiving ground would no longer be the best way to be close to Him.

Why must you exist so close to suffering? She would ask God. But He only came to her once as He did so often with Eddie or Aaron or those at church. Naomi lacked faith and resilience to suffer as she must to reunite with the Lord. And she's now thankful for that. But that doesn't change the loneliness she felt as a little girl who just wanted her mama to ask her father to stop or for her brother to hold her hand.

Naomi looks away from her mama and trudges through the muddied and dense forest to the graveyard. There is an assortment of headstones from every era of the town's existence. Some have crumbled to nothing, replaced by a concrete brick with roughly the same information. Others display a family's wealth in comparison to the rest of the humble town. The oldest is a dark obelisk erected for the death of two of Blaire's founders — Kenneth and Madeline Weir — which stands taller than the rest. Its markings illegible.

She can see her father's stone clearly, surrounded by the last of the pallbearers who wipe their brows with soiled handkerchiefs. It's a large cross made of stormy gray granite. He rests beside his father and mother. It reads nearly the same as the plaque inside except for one addition:

Naomi decides to make this quick no matter what so that she doesn't have to look at that motherfucking lie on the headstone again for the rest of her life.

"Hey, Aaron," her voice cracks, and the men look over at her. The other pallbearers pat Aaron on the back and say their goodbyes, before heading back to the church and their cars. One lays a large hairy hand on her shoulder before muttering "Sorry for your loss" to her as he passes. Her no-longer-little brother remains at the open grave. "They all leave you to bury him? Ain't that part of their job, too?"

She tries to make it sound joking. It's been too long since she knew how to speak to her brother. There was a time when they were nearly two sides of the same coin. They bathed together and shared a bike, scraped knees, and the effort it took to hide their bruise-like purple fingers from picking wild blackberries. But the two siblings both grew heavy with the weight of real bruises and *their* bike became *his* bike.

"I asked 'em earlier to let me do it myself. A son oughta bury his father. It's the right thing to do," he says solemnly.

"Mama's already waitin' in the car. I'll let her know she oughta wait inside."

"Thank you, Naomi."

Aaron dips down to grab the shovel at the head of the six-foot hole and begins to pour scoop after scoop of dirt on top of the casket. The beginning of a task that will leave him covered in sweat and earth for hours to come. Hours their mama will sit in the car on the schedule of another Darby man.

Despite the slight guilt that pesters her heart, Naomi cannot find an inch of interest in assisting her brother. She wants to participate in this process as little as possible. Put as little of herself into this as she can get away with. Naomi takes a few steps toward the hole's edge to look down where the corpse of her father lays. It's just a pit with a box only a mile or two from Naomi's own home. But with the permanency of this newfound situation, this six-foot hole may as well have been the bottom of the ocean.

"I'll be leavin' soon."

Aaron keeps digging but his eyes lock with hers. "I assume you don't mean the graveyard." He offers a wry, boyish smile that hints at the child she once knew.

"I'll do that when I'm done talkin' to you." She tries to form a smile back. "I should have the place cleaned 'n ready to sell soon."

"I'd appreciate that," Aaron murmurs as he buries their father deeper. "Would it be alright by you if I stop by sometime 'n look through what she left?"

Surely, there are enough decent knick-knacks to fill a box for her brother. They once cluttered the living room, though since moving in, Naomi donated most and stowed what was left in the basement. Nothing was specifically left to anyone after Grandma Dottie's death, besides the house itself. There wasn't much inside the house that was worth any money, anyway — Naomi checked.

"Yeah, that's alright. Just call ahead." A warm golden-orange light flourishes in her chest. Maybe it was, in fact, their father keeping them estranged. Perhaps all the years she'd been incarcerated in that house showed Aaron that she wanted to be there for him. For so long she has hoped he knew. "How's Mama?"

"Good. Been real quiet since Father died. She said she liked your dress."

Naomi looks down at her bruised knees and shins cut short by the red line of her funeral dress. The end is slightly frayed from where she poorly hemmed it. Maroon and mauve flowers pattern all the way up and over the top of the thin straps that hung on her athletic shoulders. She wears a forest green raincoat draped over it, and clunky black work boots on her feet — cleaned the night before so as not to track mud into the place of worship.

"Didn't think she talked 'bout me much." *What did Mama like about my dress? The flowers? The colors? That she couldn't see the scandalous straps?*

"She doesn't." Aaron plants the sharp tip of the shovel in the ground next to him and rests his elbow on the top of the handle. "She had to make that call the day you moved to Grandma Dottie's house. But I'm not tryin' to be one more stormy cloud today."

Oh.

Naomi bristles. Her father is still good at digging his claws under her skin even after his death. "Damn right, I moved out. Stupid small town with a bunch of snoopy assholes that go to the reverend every time you put a toe outta line. No thanks. I did my time, little brother."

Aaron sighs. He wipes his lips with the elbow of his shirt to keep the briny taste of work out of his mouth. "I didn't mean it like that, Naomi. I was kiddin'. You take things too seriously. 'Sides, this is our home. You oughta be nicer to it."

"I'm not gettin' into this fuckin' shit with you. This was it. I'll put a fuckin' postcard in a box of shit and just drop it off and you can do whatever you want to with it." Naomi turns and begins to storm out. The sound of a shovel in loose dirt makes her pause. She looks over her shoulder. "I am sorry you gotta do this on your own."

Aaron laughs and keeps up his work. "That's the difference between us, sister. I ain't ever alone. The Lord is with me every minute of every day. And now so is Father. I hope you find 'em all soon, sister, so you won't be alone neither."

This scares Naomi more than anything has in a long while. The man is dead. This is freedom. Naomi doesn't need or want to keep company with his soul. She walks out of the graveyard as fast as she can on the uneven ground. *For me*, she thinks, *he is gone 'n I am free 'n my brother has fuckin' Stockholm Syndrome for Father 'n some fucked up God. Goddamn your eyes, Aaron. Fuck you 'n all of 'em.*

Naomi enters the weed-ridden parking lot. The only vehicles left are her navy-blue truck and the sedan that still holds her mama. *Her too.*

"I love you, sister!" Aaron calls through the trees.

That hurt most of all.

When Dottie Curtis died, she left her white two-bedroom farmhouse in Naomi's name. Two stories with a covered porch out front and a large fenced-in garden. Until Grandma Dottie's death, the garden was lush and lively with cucumbers, blackberries, strawberries, squash, watermelon, and whatever other seeds she could get her hands on any given year. It grew plentiful from her sweat and tears for decades. However, Naomi's sweat and tears don't seem to have the same nutritious effect. It's now a brambly jungle of thorns and spiderwebs, impossible to walk through.

The garden was once at the center of a good deal of speculation regarding the Curtis family. Dottie's mama and daddy had practiced many Ozark folkways, or their personal version of it. Despite what that seemed to mean to the more religiously inclined townsfolk, they didn't go around on broomsticks hexing children or sacrificing goats. To many of those living in these hills, Bible verses were incantations and many of the native plants had healing properties. The traditions were an amalgamation of herbal medicine, folklore, Christianity, and Indigenous knowledge.

The talk of hexes and sacrifices were stories that only caught up to Naomi as a girl through the rumors spread by parents and then overheard by schoolmates.

"I heard Naomi's mamaw's a witch. My daddy says she put a curse on the reverend's kids 'n that's why Naomi's so weird!"

In her youth, Naomi felt that if she could be seen more as Eddie's daughter and less Dottie's granddaughter, perhaps there would be more opportunities at recess. As she grew older and less reverent of her father, she began to revel in these fables of her "mamaw" and her witchy ways.

What little she knows about Grandma Dottie's actual folk practices are only the small things so ingrained in the Ozark culture of Blaire that they don't seem godly or sinful — just the way things are.

Nowadays, the old woman's home doesn't quite feel like her own, but it is a reprieve from the outside world — from a day like today.

Naomi pulls her dress overhead and tosses it to the floor as soon as she steps through the door. She's enjoyed nakedness since living on her own. It was a freedom she never had growing up. Nudity could not be separated from sexuality and, therefore, sin. Not even for children.

It's a point of pride for Naomi that she can embrace aspects of her body, even in public, that were once seen as embarrassing or sinful. Her work at Davis's Float Rental — the neighboring town's canoe rental shop on the Kemiwe River, didn't mind. After all, work attire can be quite lax when all of the customers were drunk or preparing to get drunk.

The living room is filled with both Naomi's belongings and the last boxes of Grandma Dottie's. Fixing a box for Aaron and donating the rest are on her list of tasks before she's free to go. She has worked slowly for the past twelve years rebuilding and remodeling the property. The home deserved to be loved as it once had. Even if it wasn't by her or someone in the family line.

She often wonders if Grandma Dottie would be hurt if she knew Naomi was selling the home to an outsider. Property is everything in a family that's felt poverty breathing down their neck for so long.

Naomi's long earthen legs pull into a bow beneath her on the couch. A green plastic tray sits on the side table and she gently places it in her lap. On it is all of her paraphernalia, including a glass storage jar, cloudy from years of use. Her nimble fingers roll a joint, then she moves outside to the porch.

Joints are Naomi's favorite method for getting high. She learned to roll from Erica, who used to manage the grocery store in Mountain Springs she worked at out of high school. The woman was in her late forties and always had the wildest stories of the concerts she'd once attended — and the bandmates and roadies she slept with — from Mobile to

Chicago. Erica had been in her teens during the late eighties and lived a life governed only by herself and the law that she occasionally collided with.

When Erica found herself back home, her summers were spent at Camp Indigo — a campground on the Kemiwe open from the seventies to the nineties. It was known for its rambunctious floats down the river and the constant flow of drugs. After years of marshal and park ranger interruptions, and an uncountable number of assaults and overdoses, the camp was bought for more family-friendly purposes. That was about the time that Erica decided to (mostly) sober up.

The years of wild juvenescence caught up to her, and she had just started to allow gray to climb down from her roots when Naomi was hired at the grocery store. Although Erica had stopped her hard drug and alcohol use, she still smoked weed and introduced it to Naomi. It started as something Naomi only did after her shifts with the older woman, her friend. Since Naomi didn't have her truck at the time, she would wait for Erica to finish her managerial work so she could get a ride home.

Erica died in a car crash a year after Naomi started there. But for that while, Naomi felt a bit more comfortable with where she was in the world. After the accident, she found that she didn't want to kick the smoking habit she shared with her closest friend. Each morning, noon, and night that she inhales that sweet skunky aroma, she feels a little closer to the love and companionship that she's sought for the entirety of her life.

Sometimes the wake-and-bake feels like snuggling a lover while the sun creeps further across the floor with each passing hour. Sometimes those midday bong rips are like sharing mimosas and appetizers with a friend at a cute restaurant in a big city like in the movies. And sometimes at night when she sits on the porch with a joint between her fingers and one behind her ear — as Erica so often did — it feels like being cradled in a rocking chair and then carried to bed by a mother that loves her.

That's the love she seeks after a day of being plunged into the cold, stormy sea of familial bullshit. So, she sits in her little brown rocking chair on the front porch, lights up, holds herself tightly in her own arms, and rocks.

Once the joint begins to burn her lips, Naomi drags herself inside. As always, she locks the door behind her and pulls the curtains closed over the windows. No family portraits adorn the walls. There's little to no decoration in the home at all, with the exception of a wooden cross hanging above Naomi's bedroom door. It hasn't moved since before Naomi's arrival at the house. Grandma Dottie likely placed it there for protection, but what has a cross ever protected Naomi from?

With a stepping stool, she finally slips it off the nail. The cross is cold and dusty with disregard. She tosses it toward a stack of dark blankets bound for the thrift store and it cracks against the wall before settling. The impact leaves something slightly exposed at the bottom.

Naomi spies a penny-sized hole leading up into the shaft with a torn piece of paper stuck inside. Wary, she pulls it out and reads the faded blue script:

*"Who will establish you
and guard you from the evil one"*

She tucks the paper snuggly back inside the wood, marches down the stairs, and out the front door, and hurls the cross over her garden into the woods. Perhaps within the next few years, the bugs and elements will devour the offering for the greater good of the earth, just like her father's flesh.

The weight of the day has rested on her shoulders for hours. Paired with the THC in her system, her eyes droop and her feet are sluggish. Back inside, Naomi pops open all three windows in her bedroom to let in the cool night air. As she drops onto the mattress, it creaks from the age of the box springs Grandma Dottie and Grandpa Richard likely bought sometime in the seventies or eighties. She brings the edge of the quilt up to her chin and pulls the bedside lamp's brass string to turn it off.

Naomi is left in the subtle glow of moonlight that filters through the translucent curtains fluttering in the breeze. The smell of rain fills the room.

Chapter Three

Davis's Float Rental is a small shop on a half-acre of river frontage property. It was built in the late 1970s and hasn't been updated since. The wood siding's blue paint has chipped away, and the gas pump is an American relic. Inside are glass refrigerators with soda and beer, a freezer of ice cream and bags of ice, and an assortment of floating essentials. There are many like it on the riverway and hundreds of others in southern Missouri and northern Arkansas, but this one is Naomi's.

The sixty-two-mile Kemiwe isn't as populated by floaters as the longer Niangua, or as warm in the summertime as the Jacks Fork, or crystal clear and cold as the Current. Being smaller and less crowded is what initially led Naomi to favor it.

Naomi started her job at the shop a few years prior. The position mostly consisted of helping with equipment rentals, cleaning the lobby, and selling beer. About once a day she would load up the white van out front with kayakers, canoers, and drunk folks in inner tubes. She would hoist the equipment onto the trailer and drive everyone upstream to begin their float. It was a quiet job that did not require much human interaction outside of a cordial relationship with the manager and some drunken chatter with cheerfully sunburnt river rats. However, Naomi quit the day her father died.

Today, she visits for leisure. A pitstop before she goes to the hardware store for paint. Ryan, Naomi's old co-worker and plug, stands in the dusty gravel of the lot smoking a cigarette. The young man's dirty blond hair always curls in the summer heat, making him look younger than he is. His loose moss green "Davis's Float Rental" t-shirt collects a collar of sweat.

"Long time no see," he calls. He turns his back on her to walk through the front door covered in advertisements all the way from Blaire to Branson. Naomi follows and hums a light response.

"You gonna miss a canoe this mornin'?" Naomi asks.

"Don't think so." The blonde boy faces her from behind the counter and grabs the storage lock keys with their neon orange floaty. He tosses them to Naomi's waiting hands. "You lookin' to buy?" He raises his eyebrows suggestively.

Naomi looks around at the two glass refrigerators debating whether or not to buy some water. She lays forty dollars and a bottle on the counter. "You got any tabs?"

"Sure do. My own private stash." From the freezer, he pulls a tube of tinfoil wrapped around a sheet of acid tabs. He carefully cuts one off. The miniature smiley face printed on it peers up at her.

"I'll pick it up when I get back. 'Bout an hour or so." She nods to him before leaving.

"No worries!" Ryan replies. "There's a party comin' back in 'bout three hours or so. If you go more than half a mile up, you'll see 'em 'fore I do."

Naomi unlocks the tall storage rack that holds eight long canoes. The one she takes, *The Davis* as it has been dubbed, is nicer than the others and used exclusively by employees. When the owner passed, his family donated it to the shop to honor the old-timer. On its sides, they painted "The Davis — Kemiwe River Put-In."

The haul to the water is downhill and well-worn from thousands of pulls just like it. A large divot has been dug from canoe after canoe slicing through the mud down the embankment.

A familiar feeling washes over Naomi. The same feeling she gets each time she steps foot in the Kemiwe. The river is different from the rest of the town. Even her own home has never been her own. It was Grandma Dottie's and Naomi is just fixing it up. However, at the water, she rarely sees people from town as they favor other nearby and more popular courses.

The Darby family almost never ventured out to the river unless there was a baptism. Many prefer rowdy trips to Lake of the Ozarks rather than the gentle waves of the Kemiwe. Most of the river's visitors are old men from the area who seek the solace of the shallower waters or young folk looking for somewhere quiet to get hammered.

Hot toes meet cool water as Naomi wades in up to her calves. They curl around the weathered rocks beneath the soles of her feet. Due to almost complete deforestation in the century and a half prior, the rivers lost much of their depth and gained an all-rock bottom which allows the waterways to be crystal clear in shallower areas. It builds to a gentle teal as the water layers upon itself and becomes a hue as gorgeous as the ocean.

With expertise mastered over the years, Naomi steps into the rocking canoe and paddles upstream against the eternal current. She doesn't have a goal, really. Since her father's death, there's been a break in her routine which leaves her feeling vulnerable. Frustration has built within her, like a street cat with a BB forever embedded in its hindquarters and always on the lookout for the teen boy with a barrel in his hand. Naomi can't quite make sense of it. The boy with the BB gun is gone. The cat oughta be laid out on a hot rock with a few fish at her side, tummy fat and sunbaked, whiskers turned up in a lax smile.

My father is dead 'n I shouldn't feel like this anymore, Naomi thinks for the second time this week.

But she does, so she keeps rowing.

Deep emerald clouds of oak leaves glow overhead in the bright light of the August sun. The tops of the trees sway in a delicate summer breeze. It doesn't do much to temper the sweltering rays of sun, but the quivering of the leaves is a comforting sound. The Ozark canopy is lush this time of year and casts a shadow over the forest floor and banks of the Kemiwe that nearly make mid-morning look like evening. The black fifty-foot cliffs on the west side add to the sense that it is later than it truly is.

Naomi lays the paddle in her lap and begins to slowly coast through a narrow curve with trees joining hands overhead. However, all at once the echoing harmony of the forest dissipates and she finds herself in a silence she hasn't allowed herself to experience in the past week. All that can be heard is the shake of the leaves overhead. A death rattle of green that will soon brown and fall to the ground and leave the town exposed to the freezing winds of fall and winter.

Naomi moves to kneel on the base of the craft. With her weight shifted from her bottom to her knees, she is poised like a cottonmouth ready to strike. But a hush surrounds her and she is more like prey than predator.

This change in the atmosphere is caused by *something* that wasn't around when she left Ryan. Or it was and she'd let her guard down. Like every large expanse of wilderness, there are stories of many things that stalk between the trees. It's easy to get lost in thoughts of bears or hoop snakes, or worst of all — people.

Naomi's sight is trained on the sun-bleached rocky edge of the water as small waves beat against them. Wisps of moss dance against the shore to the water's imitation of tinkling bells.

Lap, lap, lap, SNAP. Naomi's head whips to look where the sound of a twig breaks, focusing her fear in a single direction: ahead. *Deer, raccoon, rabbit, bobcat, bear.* The possibilities fly through her thoughts like arrows.

I oughta get away from the shore. I'm too close. Someone could rush me 'n get on the canoe faster than I can get away. What if—

The canoe jolts and casts Naomi over the side to the azure water below. It rushes up her nose as she waves wildly with her arms to circle around and get her head above the surface. Her feet kick as if she's fighting an underwater assailant. But she doesn't touch a rocky bottom. Her fingertips don't reach air. *Where the fuck is the surface? It was just a fall. I can't be that far underwater. I can't be.*

Naomi opens her eyes and can't see the shadow of the canoe or the bright beacon of the sun. All there is around her is deep navy nothingness in every direction. Her limbs continue to windmill and panic sets in. She's surrounded by an endless abyss just as silent as the surface was before she fell in. She's a speck of galactic rock in the chasm of infinite space.

Then tiny spots of fluorescent green begin to ignite around her. Specks of light. *Are those sun rays?* Naomi desperately swims toward them. Her lungs burn like hellfire and the urge to suck anything into them nearly overwhelms her. The spots begin to become fewer and fewer until only two remain beneath her. Pale as peridots and only a few inches apart. *Like eyes,* she thinks, and her kicking slows. *Oh God, the rays weren't real. They weren't real.*

The orbs are distant but warming stars in her astral void. Their presence is tranquil, and her thoughts wash away down the river along with her desire to fight. The charred remains of her lungs loosen and chilled water flows in to soothe their burns. Her eyes remain locked to the mystery creature at the bottom. The other eyes don't ripple or dance with the pirouettes of the current like her floating fingers do. They remain still like rocks painted with the glowing guts of lightning bugs. Around Naomi's ankle is the thin slide of a worm wind around and around, up her calf.

Suddenly, a fish swims between her and the eyes momentarily blocking her view. The brushfire within her lungs comes rushing back to her as well as the need to flee. She closes her eyes and propels herself away from the lights. The seal of the surface abruptly breaks, and she explodes into violent coughs, water and vomit erupting from her mouth like a geyser. She sucks in as much air as she can.

Her lungs sputter and bark as she struggles to take deep breaths, while her hands tremble to grip the side of the canoe with white knuckles. She pulls herself as far out of the water as she can without tipping the *Davis* and holds herself there. *Fuckin' hell, I must've been close to passing out. Holy shit.* Naomi takes a few more moments to collect herself before swimming to the far side of the river, canoe in tow.

Once Naomi's feet touch the dry, hot stones, she collapses in a heap of exhaustion and fear. The sun shines through her eyelids. *How the fuck did I miss all this light down there?* The sun has risen above the cliff since she fell in. *It all changes so quickly.*

Naomi rests for a few minutes to conquer the shock, then she slips the craft back into the water and chases the river downstream. Perched on the wooden seat, she watches the fingertips of trees fly by.

"What the fuck?" She spits but continues to breathe.

Chapter Four

The humid oven of Naomi's truck makes her soaked clothes almost pleasant. She turns on the radio and guides the pickup around curvy foothill turns. *I was supposed to go to Mountain Springs for paint.* Grandma Dottie's old garden is an unmitigated disaster, so Naomi's plan is to gut it and paint the surrounding fence. She figures that leaving a clear garden plot with a fence to keep deer out might be inviting to a homebuyer. For years, she's debated whether she ought to match the fence to the house or paint it something cheerful, something she would like to look at. *Maybe a light blue.*

However, white is supposed to be easy to sell, according to the real estate agent Naomi spoke to with growing frequency. Rita Platte works out of Springfield and has been calling daily since Naomi's father dropped dead. The woman desperately wants to drive out and take photos of the property. With renovations, the two expect a decent return on the home. With the attached five acres, storm cellar — which was a prize in such a rocky area — garden, new roof, and a brick fireplace, it ought to be a quick sell.

With every project completed, though, Naomi always seems to find another. This is a sentiment that Rita voiced to Naomi often and usually very passive-aggressively. First, it was Naomi's concern over the cleanliness of the chimney, then the poison ivy at the southern property line, now it's the garden. The wooden fence has become weathered and gray over the decades. Where there was once a sunny pine glow to them, now they more closely resemble the vacant cold of a Midwest winter.

Maybe I oughta take that tab now, buy the paint 'n get home 'fore I come up. Before she can give herself a moment to deny a good time, she reaches over to her purse in the passenger seat. Tucked in a pocket is the blotting paper wrapped in its tin foil. Carefully, she sets the foil on her thigh and opens the edges with her fingernail. On the pad of her finger, she sticks one tab and places it on her tongue to allow it to soak into her system.

Robin's egg blue is prettier than white, Naomi considers as she takes another right corner and glimpses a green SUV sitting half in her lane a moment too late. She veers left and slams on her brakes. The front of the truck whips around and drops into the ditch with a hard shake. Naomi's arms cover her face as the momentum crashes the passenger window against the rock bluff. Absolute silence suffocates the cab.

Naomi uncovers her face once the glass settles. Through the broken window, a small branch with dark green almond-shaped leaves protrudes into the truck. It stops just inches from her face. Her labored breaths are heavy enough to shake the leaves. An orb-weaver spider holds tight to one. Like the pupil of an eye, it appears to dilate as its surroundings calm. It stretches its spindly legs wide, then descends into the truck. Naomi tries to push herself away from the spider, but she quickly withdraws her hands when they are pierced with glass.

Cradling them close to her, she looks down to find several cuts with streaks of blood between them, like their own spiderweb, and one small shard of glass in the center of her right palm. Naomi turns to find the other car, to find a way out and away from that *damn* spider. She can finally make out who is in the SUV. An unfamiliar woman sits shocked in the passenger seat while a mustached man is already out of the driver's seat and jogging to Naomi.

"Holy shit! You alright?" He raps on the glass of the window with his knuckles.

Naomi lifts her hands up to show him that she can't open her door herself. The strange man opens her door and takes her by the elbow. She wiggles her bottom until she is able to fall off the seat with unsure feet on the ground.

"Hey, lady. Are you alright?" He repeats.

"I got glass in my hands," Naomi says dryly. Again, she lifts her hands up. *Goddamn your eyes*, she thinks.

"Ah, shit this was an accident. My girl and I were talkin' about directions, and we stopped 'fore we went further. We didn't think anybody'd come by for a while. And then... there you were." The man speaks quickly. His accent is stretched and uneven. Naomi immediately notices that he isn't from the area, but she can't quite identify *where* he might be from. His speech is a patchwork of Tennessee, Texas, and Georgia. Like he's watched far too many cowboy movies and strings together a necklace of voices from his favorite characters.

"I'm Ethan Wilder, by the way," he extends his hand to her. Naomi stares at it, dumbfounded that he keeps forgetting about her hands. "Yeah… Sorry." He pulls away and wipes his undoubtedly sweaty palms on his tight jeans. She glances back at the bruised truck. "The car really was an accident. I'm a decent mechanic, actually. You know I'd be happy to tow your truck to our place and fix it up. You know, just makin' things."

Naomi's eyes track back to Ethan. He stands tall with hands on his hips, a toothy smile across his face, and fitted Wranglers which give him a boyish, country look. The look of someone who grew up watching country music videos in the mid-2000s but has never *actually* been anywhere more rural than the St. Louis suburbs. The kind of guy that inspires all the married women in a small town to be free on the day their car needs an oil change. Naomi's gaze shifts to the woman in the car. She paws at one of her eyes like something is in it. *Is she crying?*

"I don't know you two," Naomi quietly says. In a town as small as Blaire, it's difficult to meet new folks. The couple appears to be roughly the same age as Naomi. Ethan perhaps a few years older, the woman maybe younger. A bit of gray speckles his temples in otherwise dark wavy hair, and handsome crinkles branch out from his earth-toned eyes when he smiles. The woman in the SUV wears a red dress. Her golden shoulders are on display with freckles splashed like the milky way across her chest and collarbones. Sprinkles of warm copper stars dot the tops of her breasts. The woman's hair surrounds her face like a sunlit halo with waves tucked behind her ears.

"Oh! Well, again, I'm Ethan. I'm the new marshal. That's my wife, Clara," Ethan says and gestures to the golden lady in the SUV. Clara sees Ethan's thumb pointed to her and sits up straighter. Her eyes lock with Naomi, who raises her bloody hand as a hello. Clara frowns at the glass cuts on Naomi's palm. She looks as if she's going to start crying again but she still lifts her hand in greeting.

So, this is one of the men who'll replace my father, Naomi thinks distastefully, already writing him off as no good.

"We moved in about a week ago to the uh — I think his name was Tim Wallace? — Yeah, Tim Wallace's old place. Brown one off Spring." Ethan speaks far past a proper stopping point, as is common in the Midwest, but undesirable given the circumstance.

"Tim Willis," Naomi mutters. It dawns on Naomi that her bag is still in the car. The worn-soft brown satchel still sits on the floor. She taps her knuckles on the door. "You open this for me?"

"For sure." Ethan steps forward and pulls the door open. The spider is nowhere to be seen. Naomi carefully leans over the seats. The glass scrapes her shirt as she reaches for the floor on the passenger side. She hooks her least-damaged finger under the shoulder strap and pulls it to her. As she scoots out, she spies the tin foil by the gas pedal. Ever so carefully and discreetly, she plucks it from the floor and tucks it into the purse.

Ethan looms over the driver's side door with hips cocked and a hand resting at the top of the cab. He hovers like a mosquito.

"Well, like I said, I'd be happy to get this fixed for you myself. I gotta pick the tow truck up from the house. Clara can get you somethin' to eat while you wait." Ethan steps towards his SUV. He opens the driver's side door and sticks his head in to mumble something to Clara. The golden woman steps out of her side onto the gravel road. She smiles at Naomi, and it is just as sunny as the rest of her. A thin pale line is etched from the cleft of her chin to two inches below the corner of her lip. A newer scar freshly healed. Naomi walks around her to the back passenger side. Clara opens the door for her, and Naomi offers an awkward smile back.

"I just live down the way, 'bout a mile from here." Naomi hopes he will take the hint that she would much rather get dropped off at her own house.

Instead, he guffaws and insists. No music plays but the A/C storms its way through to the backseat. The trip only takes a few minutes. A cloud of dust follows them to the couple's home about a mile from Naomi's place. She figures she can walk it with relative ease if she waits until dusk to avoid the heat. The mosquitos will be a bitch, but it will be quiet. *Quiet sounds nice.*

The Wilder's home is a wood cabin with a dark teal door. Naomi figures this is a new addition since it doesn't quite fit the dead old man's simple aesthetic. As they make their way toward the cabin, Clara's red dress sways in the summer breeze. Naomi wonders how soft the fabric is.

"Alright ladies, I'm gonna get the tow truck. You'll be alright for a while, Clara?"

Clara hums a gentle response. Ethan smiles widely and backs away a few steps before winking at his wife. His keys dangle from his front belt loop and jangle loudly as he saunters away. The two women stand in uncomfortable silence. Naomi looks down to assess the damage to her hands. They sting, worse than they did on the ride over. Adrenaline can only work its magic for so long.

"Oh, I'm so sorry. I forgot you were hurt. You can follow me, and I'll get those cleaned up." Clara's voice is soft and doesn't carry the same accented lilt of her husband. Naomi's silently grateful neither offered to take her to a clinic. Any damage she collected as a child was rubbed with dirt and walked off. The habit hasn't been given a good reason to die just yet.

Clara's dress sashays through the entryway, living room, and up the pine stairs to the main bathroom where she busies herself with drugstore medical supplies beside an antique clawfoot tub. Clara gestures for Naomi to sit on the toilet seat. The injured woman splays the back of her hands against the top of her thighs.

Clara digs through a wicker basket beside the toilet and withdraws an antiseptic liquid, gauze, wrap bandages, and rubbing alcohol. She plugs up the sink and fills it with steaming water before adding about half a cup of alcohol. Naomi isn't familiar enough with at-home medicine to know if her makeshift doctor's methods are sound.

Clara kneels in front of her and a shine begins to stretch from Naomi's heart to the tips of her fingers. It tickles and sparkles under the sensitive skin of her inner hands and dances along the outlines of her abrasions. It's a nervous, delighted energy that has been long dormant in some cave inside her.

Naomi's sweaty and dirty and exhausted. She likely smells of fish and sunscreen, but the woman that sits below her doesn't squish her nose in distaste or spritz the eucalyptus-scented bathroom spray. The weight of Naomi's guilt settles over her like a rockslide. *What am I supposed to do? I swerved the car. Maybe I coulda braked in time if I hadn't swerved like a jackass. I did this 'n now I'm in debt.*

Clara gently collects Naomi's right hand into her own and examines the glass shard that protrudes from the center. It's a tiny piece — half an inch at most — but she keeps her fingers on the outskirts of her palm so as not to sting the worst of the cuts. Clara's hands are nimble and kind. She doesn't speak much as she cleans and wraps, and Naomi finds herself wondering if she works in the medical field. And if she notices the scabs that line Naomi's fingernails.

"I hope you don't need to use these anytime soon." Clara lifts her eyes to look through her lashes.

"I'll be alright." Naomi pulls her bandaged right hand into her chest. "You do this often?"

"No. Sometimes Ethan will get a cut or need some ice while he's working in the garage. I don't really know what I'm doing." The golden girl is nervous and so is she.

It's easier for Naomi to exist around women. It always has been. Often, she still wishes she could just *pop* in and out of existence. However, around those of her same sex, the agony of awaiting that disappearance isn't gnawing teeth at her skin.

"Coulda fooled me," Naomi jokes in an attempt to make the woman a tad more comfortable. Clara's nervous eyes dart here and there, and her weight's perched upon her knees. The tile probably leaves indentations. The cuts on Naomi's hands burn. She thinks about an alternate version of this scenario where she went to her own home to care for these. She prefers her current and much prettier company.

"We have some leftovers if you want any. And some lemonade?" Clara raises herself from the floor and drops the supplies into the sink. Blood swirls like smoke in the still water. Deep rouge softening into a rose-tinted pool. Naomi examines her patched hands. The gauze wraps around her palms and weaves between her fingers in order to keep Clara's fine work in place. Naomi follows suit after her nurse and flips the light switch off with her elbow.

"Alright."

Chapter Five

The night before, the couple dined on lasagna. It's a dish that Naomi has only indulged in once before. Growing up, the cost of the cheese that lasagna requires was too lavish for the Darby's. Spaghetti was as far into Italian cuisine as the penny-pinching family ventured. But the dish in front of Naomi consists of tomato sauce with ingredients that Clara said were from her garden. Mozzarella stretches and rolls over its edges. The top is crunchy with garlic breadcrumbs, golden brown from their time broiling in the oven. Layers of large basil leaves — also homegrown — lie beneath each layer of cheese. Naomi stops herself after a single bite.

Oh my God. Unsure if it's an honest sensation or if the acid is kicking in, it's the greatest bite of food she has ever tasted.

"Oh, I meant to ask if you wanted dry clothes," Clara covers her mouth while she speaks around the half-chewed food.

Naomi pauses, unsure of what Clara is referring to. Her first concern is if she pissed herself during the accident. She shifts, buttock to buttock, and then she understands. *I fell in the goddamn river.*

Naomi begins to laugh. "I've had the most goddamn ridiculous day. It's alright. Just water." She can't keep her smile under wraps.

"Oh, do you like to swim?" Clara's eyes blow wide with curiosity.

Naomi pauses. She doesn't want to tell this stranger a story that might make her consider if her dinner companion has lost her mind. *Hell, it could even make me liable.* The event spooked her but, retrospectively, she wonders if she even remembers it properly. Maybe the stress of almost drowning, then getting into a car accident has fried her brain. Those glowing green spheres of light are still stuck in Naomi's mind like a shitty commercial jingle. *They looked so much like sun rays…*

"Uh yeah. I used to work at the Put-In. Davis's on the Kemiwe." Naomi takes a bite and speaks with lasagna blocking her tongue. "You?"

Clara smiles shyly. "No, I never learned."

"I still got access to the shop's employee canoe. We could go sometime 'n I could teach you." The proposal releases a flood of apprehension in Naomi's gut. There is a pull towards Clara, but she can't tell if her tablemate feels it too. And she knows it's very unlikely that Clara is experiencing it in the same way she does. It's been a long time since the lonely woman had a friend. Not since Erica.

That had been years ago. Perhaps she doesn't remember how it's supposed to start. Slow or all at once.

Clara's eyes light up. "I'd like that! You know, we haven't been here long — just a few days — but we don't really know anyone yet. It'd be nice to do something out of the house."

Maybe Clara does feel the same way.

An hour passes rapidly as the two women hit it off. Naomi's clothes dry from the heat of her body and the setting sun. They hold the scent of humid summer air and sweat. She worries that Clara will catch a waft and want her out. She needs to leave soon. *It's for the best*, Naomi thinks. *Visuals are gonna kick in soon. Paranoia's already here. I oughta not fuck this up.*

The two women stand side by side at the kitchen sink with their dishes. Clara washes and Naomi dries. It's a silent, relaxing chore. Naomi admires the care with which Clara handles her dishes and silverware. Adept fingers scrub every nook and cranny before she passes off the dripping dish to Naomi. The droplets of water roll down each dish in an effort to catch the one before it.

The window above the sink frames the backyard. The sun starts to set but in the dusky light, Naomi spies the cultivated beauty of a garden. It seems to grow as she watches. Like her gaze gives the patch an audience to perform for. The vines and stems grow and sway to music Naomi can't quite hear. But even so, the allurement of the garden stretches like an aura of hands toward her. To pull her into their prism of magic.

"You got the garden goin' that quick?" Naomi nods her chin toward the patch.

"It belonged to the man we bought the place from. Tim Willis, you said? He hadn't maintained it for a few years. Just let it keep growing. So, I've been working to get a handle on it." Clara hands her another fork. "I brought a few plants with us, too."

"So, you... like gardenin'?" Naomi curses herself for being so socially fatigued this soon into an interaction. She feels the weight of her words like they are bogged down with water. The otherworldly allure of the garden pulls away from her. She isn't quite allowed into its ethereal plane.

Naomi wonders how much work she has put into the small plot in such a short amount of time. It's hard to tell that anything's been done to the jungle. "Yep. It's nice not having to go to the store. Some sustainability, some self-reliance." She looks back down at her hands in the steaming sink water.

"If you're interested, I might have a garden you could fix up." Naomi immediately catches that her invitation sounds like she's trying to hire Clara. Her request was supposed to be more personable. "I mean, I'm tryin' to get my place a little... nicer. My thumb ain't exactly green. So, if you want, you could come over 'n teach me."

Clara turns off the faucet and takes the dish towel out of Naomi's hands. She dries her own and places it on the counter. "You teach me to swim; I teach you to keep your garden alive? I can do that. There are a few things we can grow in the fall. Soon would be a great time to start." A small glass jar of toothpicks is perched between two houseplants on the window's ledge. Clara slips one between her teeth.

The idea warms Naomi, but she doesn't plan on staying long enough to enjoy even a fall harvest. She mumbles a reticent thank you. "I oughta head out now. Thanks for your hospitality. Could I thank him 'fore I leave? For fixin' the truck." Naomi grabs her bag off the coat rack and tosses it over her shoulder.

Clara opens the front door and ushers her to the porch. She looks toward the backside of the property. "That rusty thing on the other side of the garden is the garage. That's where he is." Clara stands at the top of the stairs as Naomi walks down.

"Thank you very much for everythin' today. That was the best meal I've had in a while." Naomi wrings her hands and hopes that she is able to convey her sincerity.

"You're welcome. And I'm very serious about the swimming lessons," Clara says wryly. The toothpick rests at the corner of her mouth where her lips curl up in an affectionate smirk.

"And I'm serious 'bout the gardenin' lessons." Naomi turns and strolls to the garage.

The intrusive thoughts begin as soon as Clara isn't in her eye line. *Was I funny enough? Did I seem rude?* Naomi has always easily collapsed into a hole inside her own head. Falling prey to the cruelty of her own thoughts is usual when the only company she has is her own. The charity that Ethan and Clara have shown her is greater than any she's received in years. It overwhelms her and nearly sets her into fight-or-flight.

The light of the moon isn't yet above the trees. But the glowing fluorescents of the barn creep closer and closer until they illuminate Naomi's path. They are a vibrating chartreuse glow to her drugged senses. Like the light, it belongs to a breathing creature above, benevolent enough to shed its light on those below.

She can see her old faithful truck with a jack underneath. The damage is just as bad as she remembers it. Undrivable but perhaps fixable. There's a lit cigarette smoking from a tin can beside the truck.

"Uh hi," Naomi calls to the boots sticking out from under the hood. The boots jump, and Ethan thunks his head on the bottom of the truck with a shout of "shit!"

He slides out from under the vehicle on his mechanic's creeper. He sits upright with his thighs spread wide and arms resting on his knees.

With a rag, he wipes his sweaty brow and the black fuzzy caterpillar wriggling above his lip curls to one side in a smirk that mirrors his wife just minutes before. Upon a closer look, his eyes seem to grow in size. Larger and larger until they eclipse most of his face in two black holes destined to swallow him entirely. Naomi looks away before she is swept up in the gruesome imagery of her trip.

"You scared the hell outta me," Ethan points at her. "But I got good news for you." The man stands. "All the damage is positively rectifiable. I can do it here, too, for free. Since we were also involved in this mess. I'll work on your truck every free minute I have. It should be done in… two weeks? Three maybe?"

Well, shit. That time frame put a damper on her plans.

"Uh, thank you. For everythin'," Naomi responds.

"For sure! We're neighbors," Ethan smiles brightly before he sits back down on the creeper and pushes himself under the truck once more.

Chapter Six

Naomi dismissed Clara's concerns about her walk home. Clara pressed that Naomi could have asked Ethan, but it was too much. Too much help, too much kindness, too much debt. It's easier to walk herself home. The return won't be bad — especially now that the sun is down, and the atmosphere is humid but only gently warm. A glisten still appears on her skin, but it's swept over by a light breeze that makes walking enjoyable. *'Sides, a walk in nature with acid on the brain? Good a time as any*, she thinks.

Once Naomi reaches the main road, she looks back to see if the cabin is still in sight. The canopy of trees behind her and the canopy ahead of her is all that's left. Like a snake has swallowed her whole. She's in the belly of the beast with nowhere to go but forward. The trees shimmy in the wind like a gentle tambourine overhead. *Or maybe that's the acid.*

The glow of moonlight occasionally sneaks its way to the ground, but most of her light comes from the flashlight Clara loaned her on the way out. The light illuminates the clusters of spiderwebs that have collected on the trees.

Beetles and moths dart across the flashlight. They flutter over Naomi's hand and face as she bats them away. She digs into her purse and finds a painkiller bottle filled with a single joint and a mini-lighter. She pauses to light up. One drag after another. Every inhale gets her a little higher until she is able to look down at her day with a new perspective. Like an out-of-body experience. Only then does she resume her mile-long trek back home.

All things considered, the day was shit. She nearly drowned in the river, she ran her truck into a bluff, and now she's being swarmed by light-hungry bugs. There hasn't been time to process the events. It was her first car accident. Thirty years without one is likely defying some sort of odds but she doesn't find comfort in that. It was scary and she feels largely to blame for it all. She could have hit the brakes and stopped in time. *I made it complicated*, Naomi fixates. *I nearly knocked 'em off the road.*

But you didn't. You got to meet somebody new, a kinder voice within her comforts. *And nice 'n pretty.*

It isn't the best timing in the world, with the for-sale sign waiting to be erected in her front yard. *It would be a nice note to leave on.* Maybe she will even have a healthy root that plants itself into the soil of Blaire before she leaves. It's a lovely sentiment to have something good left in her hometown. Naomi doesn't want her entire existence in Blaire to be gone in the time it takes to drive to the next town.

It would be nice if there was somethin' left of me here.

Clara was generous and thoughtful. It felt comfortable sitting with this new person at the dinner table. *Like two girlfriends at brunch in the city. And Clara said we'd do it again. Hell, the truck's gonna take a few weeks. And she's gonna teach me about the garden. And I'm gonna teach her to swim.* It's easy to get caught up in something so new.

Naomi thinks back to the moment earlier with her when she was reminded of Erica. The ache of lost friendship often stings worse than the loss of her family. One night, not long before Erica's fatal car accident, Naomi sat with knees to her chest as some classic rock ballad played on the radio. A band Erica had fucked her way through. She'd had a way of recounting the stories every time one of these familiar groups played.

Erica was quiet that evening, not bothering to repeat the story of her Eiffel Tower with the drummer and bassist of the prog-rock band that echoed through the car. She was beautiful. Long blonde and gray curls. The coils often lightly knotted together in what the woman called faerie curls — a term that thrilled Naomi due to its forbidden nature. Her past life was still very fresh, and she was working overtime to decipher legitimate morality from cruelty.

Erica's lips had thinned with age and brick-colored lipstick transferred from her mouth to the joint's filter. Naomi felt like a woman possessed by what her father would have called a demon, but what she couldn't quite name. Naomi leaned in to kiss Erica as the woman held the joint out to her. It was easy to reach for the red of her lips.

Naomi was completely inexperienced. She locked her naked lips to her dearest friend's and held her breath. Her eyes opened before she pulled back. Erica's were closed, and then opened so delicately, so dreamily, that Naomi thought perhaps her response would match. But it did not.

"Oh baby, you're too young for me." Erica took the marijuana cigarette back from Naomi's hand. She took a final drag and then snuffed it out on the side of the sedan and tucked it into the ashtray. Naomi's eyes settled on the forest outside the car. She wanted to lose herself in its heavy presence, be pressed between the thick tree trunks until her insides ran out. The flame of blush on her cheeks was stoked by an ember of fear. The booming voice of her father sounded in her head about the evils of a kiss shared outside the will of God. Her head began to throb.

"I didn't know you liked girlies, girlie." Erica looked at her with a kind and crooked smile.

"I don't," Naomi whispered.

Erica watched the girl for a moment. She must have seen the flush on her cheeks and chest. More importantly, she had previously shared her own experiences with unrequited love — if that's what this firefly kiss could be called.

"I don't know what you've been told about kissin' girls, but it ain't that I think it's wrong or even that I don't like girls, too. I've liked 'em plenty of times. But—" Erica struggled to find the words. She grabbed a fresh joint from behind her ear and slid it behind Naomi's. She gently pushed her hair back and held her cheek. "I'm just too old to be that for you. It wouldn't be right of me. Even if you did kiss me first. I can't do that to you."

At first, the memory had burned with embarrassment. But it didn't take long, days maybe, until it felt like water under the bridge. Erica was quite talented at letting things go, at not letting embarrassment smother a good thing. That kindness in Erica is a twin flame in Clara.

Naomi is surprised to find that her feet are walking up the familiar start of her own gravel drive. Her joint went out while she was lost in thought. Crunchy footsteps come to a halt while she flicks the lighter and tries to relight the tip of the joint without taking her eyelashes with it. The skunky fog fills her lungs and she breathes it out like a dragon.

But the smoke doesn't flutter away like it did earlier, and the bugs no longer hog the illumination of the flashlight. The air is as still as a forgotten old pond, and the gray waves linger in front of her. The pungent odor clings to her, same as the moisture. It's hotter and stickier now than it was only a bit ago when she initially met the main road. The leaves no longer rattle and each breath she takes is a gust of wind to her ears.

A soft fluttering of leaves begins again. The wind blows high above her like it does to signal an incoming storm. Her loud footfalls aren't a human enough sound to scare bears away, but those aren't something Naomi considers a viable danger very often. Particularly since black bears usually turn tail and run at the first sight of a person.

Naomi gazes up at the leaves overhead. They remain still although she can hear the ghostly rattle of them behind her, as if the wind hasn't caught up to her yet. She keeps walking with her eyes gazing upward, watching. She feels stupid doing it — like a turkey about to drown in the rain. But the light of a nearly full moon comes into view through an opening in the canopy and it is all so beautiful.

Maybe the storm isn't here yet, but with the leaves that shake behind her, it can't be far. *Right?* She goes to take another drag and realizes the joint is out once again.

"Goddammit."

One last time, she flicks her lighter. The yellow tip of the flame licks the burnt end. It's too short now not to burn her if she lights it from between her lips. She takes a drag and gazes at the moon, the wind nearly at her back. The leaves shake like a rattlesnake. Naomi turns and looks down the dark drive, branches rounding at the top like an underground tunnel.

In front of her, there is nothing but darkness and the knowledge that her house isn't far. But her eyes are trained on the treetops at the mouth of the wooded tunnel, away from the comfort she left behind not long ago. The leaves remain still.

Why don't I see the wind?

Then something emerges from the leaves. But it seems too slow to match what she hears. A single patch at the top of the tunnel ahead of her trembles. The other branches remain static, except for the acid-induced pulsing of life. As if a critter climbed up and is jumping from tree to tree in a straight line toward her. The rustling begins to sound less like the wind in the trees and more like something coming through the forest.

Her stare is frozen on the spot at the top of the mouth of the black road. A dark shape catches the moonlight there; something that is not a part of the trees. It barely hangs under the leaves as it continues to glide toward her. It reflects no light. It is black emptiness. Like everything could be shoved into it and forgotten all at once. The thing does not sway, just very slowly hovers toward Naomi. Even her stoned eyes tell her brain it's unnaturally still for something that is in fact moving toward her. Still, she can't move. Until it begins to take on the shape of feet.

Two knobby feet attached to thin ankles. They cut through the leaves and branches above the tunnel. Its toenails are long and caked with dirt. The skin is grayed with deep purplish veins that bulge slightly over the top of boney ankles. Each limb is longer than a human's. Like it's stretched by gravity to slowly extend itself to the earth, long and wispy like smoke. The scrawny calves are visible up to the knees. The being continues to float closer and closer. Naomi's teeth pinch the joint and her flashlight creeps up to the hanging feet.

Those are feet. They come to an abrupt stop but don't waver despite the momentum.

I'm high, I'm high, I'm high. I'm just high, she chants to herself.

Until the feet begin to slowly drop. Naomi is so shocked and captivated by the feet that she only peripherally sees, slightly above where she stares, that two green lights have flashed on above the toes. Far enough above them that she doesn't consider that they might be eyes because they are so much higher than where a person's eyes should be.

Naomi turns and sprints. The joint falls from her teeth and her feet pound the gravel again and again and again. *Oh fuck how far do I have to go? How close am I?* The sound of wind picks up much louder than before. She's close to the house but the rustling sound of the disturbed canopy is closer. The toes might be lower than before. Are they about to graze the back of her neck? Are cold fingers about to grab hold of her hair?

Naomi sees her porchlight at the end of a long dash. The wind is at her back, and she imagines it lower and lower. Naomi is a hundred feet from the front door when she thinks to find her keys. She pulls her purse up from where it bounces on her hip. One shaking hand reaches in to find them and the other holds the bag as still as she's able. She grabs the ring and starts to shuffle through the keys without looking. Her house key is smaller than the rest. She hopes she'll know it when she feels it.

Naomi passes by the garden and her grandma's pawpaw tree and the sound suddenly stops. She jumps up the steps two at a time and tries to fit the key in the lock. Her breath heaves and her eyes burn from kicked-up dust and tears. The lock clicks and she throws her body weight against the door, falling to the floor as it swings open. Naomi turns around expecting to see the thing standing in her door frame.

But it's just an empty porch and the dust of a dirt road recently used.

Naomi slams the door shut and double locks it. She wrenches every curtain in the house closed before she sits on the floor of her bedroom in front of the window and peers out at the cloud of dust on the drive already settling. The trees shroud most of the long path up to the house in shadow, but there are about forty feet before the front door that are exposed. Naomi makes sure the window and the bedroom door are locked before shuttering the final curtain and hunkering down on her bed ready for the acid to wear off.

Autumn

Chapter Seven

An awful aching in Naomi's head rips her from a heavy sleep. The room is shrouded in shadow, and she reaches blindly for the water bottle by the bed to ease her headache and dry mouth. After several deep gulps, Naomi rolls on her back and stares at the ceiling, wishing the day away. She still senses the phantom high from last night and, mixed with sleep, it makes her a foggy kind of exhausted. A throbbing pulse radiates in the balls of her feet as she stretches herself like a cat.

The feet.

The green lights.

Naomi shoots up. The darkness surrounding her suddenly suffocating. The lights could appear again in any dark corner. In a panic, she rips one side of the bedroom curtain open to expose herself to the safety of the sunlight. It's overcast, but she can still tell it isn't as early as when she usually wakes up. She uses the heel of her hand to roughly rub the sleep from her eyes. The gauze scratches gently at her skin.

Naomi can't recall exactly how she got home. The memory is intertwined with a horrible nightmare. Or maybe a bad trip. It isn't often that she has nightmares. Since she started smoking, her dreams have been less frequent. Most nights come and go without them — the good kind and the bad. Sometimes she finds it disappointing. The belief that dreams might send you to far-off beaches, or space, or send you messages and prophecies, is inviting.

But what she saw last night was visceral. The kind of vivid scene you see when you kick weed for a few days and have withdrawal dreams that are as detailed as photographs. The kind that is so bad that you don't care if they spill the secrets of the future: images of those dirty, gray feet floating through the trees. *And those goddamn lights again.* Perhaps while she was tripping, she panicked. It all went south due to how awful yesterday was, how exhausted she was. Maybe the stress and trauma got to her more than she realized. That, mixed with moving and the death of her father — it could all add up, right? Or maybe she was closer to death in that river than she thought.

Maybe it was Father's eyes. Father's ghost in the trees. If he wouldn't leave her be in death, she isn't sure what kind of life that would leave her. Would it even be worth it, then? *Shit idea to trip*, she scolds herself.

It's nearly noon when she enters her kitchen and starts cooking a fried egg breakfast. The silvery sky drizzles on the window. The heat continues to dissipate from the previous day, leaving a lush and vibrant green oasis outside. The plant life glows an electric green that only occurs when every plant has taken its fill of rainwater and now stretches its limbs to the sky in search of sunlight. The aura of life illuminates the world in a way the sun never does.

A part of her wants to lie down on the couch and do nothing. What's one more day before she escapes? Naomi saw that some channel scheduled her favorite old Western today. Or tomorrow. Maybe she can find it to stream. The lead actor was nearly a member of the family when she was little. Naomi remembers crying when she watched him die for the first time in the movie. With tears running down her face, she begged her father to tell her why he had to die. In her youthful eyes, he was noble. An American hero. Eddie explained that it happened to us all. And those old characters in their chaps and cowboy hats — above most men — died doing what was right.

"I ain't accustomed to comparin' just any man to Jesus, but like our Savior, he knew what must be done. He saved them boys, Naomi." Eddie's hand rested on her shoulder, heavy as an oak.

Seldom does her mind toss her shiny memories of her father. Many of the ones that shine feature that same old Western actor on the screen while her father lounges in his recliner, Naomi on the floor. Whatever film, it was always made in the 1970s or earlier. Naomi imagines her father saw himself in these stoic men that sought to right the wrongs of an untamed and unjust world. But she thinks these men stood too tall compared to her father. He was shadowed next to them.

With a satisfied stomach and clean plate, she brandishes a pair of rain boots, fills a bucket with water, and hauls her cleaning supplies down the rickety basement stairs. All that remains to be donated sits in boxes upstairs, which collect more junk by the day. The cellar is gray and unfinished.

Pipes and wires are exposed and give little space for head clearance, particularly for those concerned with spiderwebs. The cold concrete floor and walls are two chained handcuffs away from a slasher movie set.

With a scratchy bristled broom, she sweeps leaves and the corpses of spiders into a dustpan. The walls and corners are brushed with a duster, then scrubbed with a sponge. The underside of the steps receives the same treatment but with the duster extended to its full length for fear the spiders will drop as their homes are swept away. As much as Naomi loves the wilderness, she has never liked spiders.

On the back wall under the stairs, Naomi squats and uses both hands to wipe up and down vigorously on a patch of dirt that won't let up. A watermelon-sized inkblot of a stain remains at knee height. *Is this a burn mark?* Naomi uses her weight for extra strength as she scrubs.

Abruptly, the wall collapses beneath her hands and the sponge plunges into the darkness, where her knuckles bust into something hard. In revulsion, she pushes herself out of the crevice onto her hindquarters. Naomi looks at her hands to check for bugs or mold or whatever other disgusting things could be crawling up her arms. There's only the dust and dirt from cleaning that lingers under her nails and paints the gauze over her palms, along with the pang along her right knuckles that is sure to bloom into a bruise.

Naomi returns with a flashlight and peers into the small hole. There are no webs, only the crumblings of elderly concrete. On the ground are three antique wooden boxes. Between her cheek and shoulder, she wedges the handle of the light. She reaches in and flips the latch of the closest box. Inside are photographs and papers, yellowed with time. Naomi withdraws as many of them as her fingers can hold.

Placing the stack on the floor and returning the light to her hands, she takes a good look at her find.

It's a color photograph of Grandma Dottie in what is likely the late eighties or early nineties. Her hair is grayed, but just as long as Naomi remembers from when she was a girl. Lines sprout from her eyes like tree roots and ripple around her mouth like broken river swells. She sits on the rocking chair, a toddler seated on her lap — Naomi.

The stack alternates between photos and letters with a story about the photos. The handwriting is loopy and tight. Each word is written with care and easily legible. It's obvious that the project was a labor of love. For the photo of Naomi, its letter states that Naomi loves bananas and visits to the creek. It says the owls in the trees scare her when they hoot, but she giggles every time she sees a frog.

Naomi's throat grows tight as a noose. If she hadn't broken through this wall, they would have been lost when this house inevitably caved in or burnt down. These are details not shared by her mama or father. Information about herself that even she is not familiar with.

The next picture is of Aaron. Grandma Dottie is wearing the same red and white dress, and he's in a pair of overalls with no shirt. Its letter states that he likes pureed sweet potatoes and when Grandpa Richard plays the fiddle. He cries when he's kissed but loves to hold Grandma Dottie's finger.

Naomi doesn't think she can name four things about Aaron as he is now. She stacks the photos and information sheets in proper order and returns them to the box.

Her chest aches and her breaths are held together by the tightly bound loops of letters in Grandma Dottie's notes. She returns upstairs.

Outside, the sky still cries, and the world is in an emerald glow. She picks up her phone but pauses — Aaron deserves to see the box of treasures. He deserves this agonizing observation of the family that they were robbed of when they were so young. Surely it will mean more than Precious Moments figurines or Grandma Dottie's old ashtray. Aaron must carry similar memories of Grandma Dottie, which are sparse and clouded even for her.

As far back as Naomi can remember, she only saw her Grandma Dottie at church (when Dottie would go), Mother's Day, and Margaret's birthday. Every September 13th, Grandma Dottie would ascend the stairs of the pale gray ranch-style house that her daughter lived in. There was no garden — Eddie preferred his wife to go to the town grocer for his food. Grandma Dottie would be greeted with two small faces and four grabby hands pulling her into a million hugs in those early years. At some point during the celebration, Dottie did two things: one, get her daughter alone; and two, get her granddaughter alone.

Each year, Naomi and sometimes Aaron would listen in on their private conversation.

"Baby, you are all I have left. I live in that house all by myself," Grandma Dottie cried and held her daughter's hands as tightly as she could. Margaret stared at the wall. "I don't get to see my grandbabies but a few times a year. How many of those do I got left? Nobody knows, baby. Please, please let me in."

Margaret looked over to her mama. "God knows, Mama. You should ask Him to let you in."

Grandma Dottie refused to do so in the way that Eddie and Margaret required. She died three years after that birthday. Her tombstone at Blaire Baptist Graveyard was simple and impersonal. Grandma Dottie had no other children to execute her will.

Grandma Dottie detailed in a note found in an old desk in her basement that she wanted to be cremated and spread over her property — particularly the garden. But at the private family meeting to arrange the funeral, Eddie told Margaret that her mama only stood a chance to enter Heaven if she had a Christian burial. So, her body rotted in a corner of the church graveyard. It succumbed to the bugs and weather rather than fertilize the wilderness and the plants that were her only company in her last years. Naomi fears that, even in death, she will have no autonomy against her father's church.

Naomi isn't sure how to get ahold of Aaron. She's never needed to call her little brother. Either they lived in the same house, or they were estranged. The concern with calling the old house is that her mama could answer. And that's something that she's very stringently avoiding.

Instead, Naomi calls the church. It's an *old* institution attended by *old* people. Surely it wouldn't be in their interest to change the number and be hounded by the elderly folks in the town demanding to know why the number is different after so many decades.

"Pastor Aaron Darby. How can I help you?"

Naomi is roused from her thoughts and thrown into the reality of the situation. *Play nice,* she scolds herself.

"Uh hey, little brother."

"Naomi! I was wonderin' if I'd hear from you soon. When you didn't send me a postcard from Miami, I thought maybe there was hope!" His chuckle is a warm wave. It's nice to know he has grown into a man with humor. A man whose mouth isn't stern and bowed down. "Oh! Grandma

Joyce was just talkin' to me about some little dog that might need a home—"

"No thanks." Immediately, embarrassment fills her, head to toe, as she slips back into her nasty mood from the other day. "Sorry." Her fingers pick at one another anxiously.

When he replies, she imagines his soft smile on the other side of the line. "It's alright. There's been a lot of stress 'n loss. I forgive you." Whatever plugged her up with embarrassment is released and it oozes out and leaves Naomi lighter than the dust that floated into her hair in the basement.

The basement.

"Listen, Aaron, I found some of Grandma Dottie's ol' stuff. Some more sentimental pieces. I was wonderin' if you'd like to come by 'n look. I ain't sure it's best to split it all up but — well, we can talk 'bout that when you're here." A line of skin hangs loose beside her nail where she pulled it up, dried and irritated.

A slam on the other end of the line causes Naomi to jump out of her skin. The phone nearly slips from between her slick fingers. "That sounds real nice, Naomi. Anythin' you want me to bring? I can have Lily make a pie. Any in particular you like?"

"I dunno who Lily is." The words rush out, propelled by curiosity. She nearly bites herself in regret.

"That's my ol' lady. S'all right. You and me haven't been close in a long while. There's a lot of catchin' up to do."

Naomi sighs in relief. Each move she makes may cause her to lose. She clears her throat in an attempt to dislodge her discomfort. "What day works for you?"

"With all the changes at church 'n home, it won't be for a bit. Maybe three weeks from Friday?"

"Alright," she agrees.

Naomi imagines him penning the date down. Maybe in colorful ink so it stands out on his schedule. Something special. "And Naomi? Thank you for this."

Naomi rests the cell phone on the kitchen counter. She gathers a basket and Grandma Dottie's gardening gloves. The thirst for intimacy and recognition within her family burns stronger than it has in years. Naomi wants these feelings to be stuffed inside that box in the basement. She knows that she fooled herself into thinking that her mama and brother would run to her when Eddie was dead and gone. It was a pipe dream, fed by years of isolation and delusion and likely a dash of her own self-righteousness. But maybe there's still space for reconnection after all.

Naomi's memories of their childhood are marred by religious zealotry and abuse. A good deal of those memories take place in that five-by-eight underground room where her father put her to be punished. It was mostly filled with Mama's canned goods on rickety wooden shelves. There was no light source. A door of solid wood was centered on one wall, secured with a padlock. Floors of dirt and walls of cement made for a cold and uninviting space. In the corners were spiderwebs and it was a common hiding place for mice, rats, and snakes in the cold of winter or the drenched spring.

Eddie would grip Aaron's arm with fingers like handcuffs and drag the young boy faster than he could keep up with to the underground room. With a heavy key latched to his belt, he'd unlock it and leave the small child inside. The cellar was not checked for creatures before it was used as a cell. The boy knew better than to scream. Once the door was shut, his tears would come.

Their father would return when he felt his son was ready. The weather did not change the length of punishment. There were no pleading words from their mama to bring her son back home. Her days of advocacy for her children had long since expired.

"It's for their souls, Margaret," Eddie would say.

And when he returned to the cellar, he'd ask Aaron if God had spoken to him. This punishment started so young that Aaron likely didn't remember what his responses were at first. Only that the correct response was "Yes, sir" and a correction of what he'd done wrong.

Naomi, however, would be no church leader. In his eyes, there was no position for her in their family. She would be someone's wife, someone's mama, someone's housekeeper. Naomi could never be worthy of a spoken connection to their Lord, so the back of his hand, the belt, or a pool of grits to kneel on were used as punishment instead.

Eddie worked hard to ensure that Naomi's future husband did not need to work as hard as he did in order to produce a devoted and obedient wife. When Naomi was small, she would lay curled in bed on her side, bottom naked and molten from the leather of her father's belt and pray that she too could be put in the root cellar. *Aaron probably sits with the mice like Cinderella*, she had thought bitterly.

But that time has long since passed. So much time has passed that Naomi just had a downright *pleasant* conversation with her brother. An olive branch was extended and there's nothing to do now but move forward.

Naomi abandons her rain boots on the porch and walks barefoot to the far corner of the yard. She lets the rain fall on her nose and slips off into the dirt. Her face has no makeup, so there will be no mascara lines from the precipitation or her own tears. Weeding the massive yard will keep her occupied for a while. Long enough for the tears to stop.

Chapter Eight

The front lawn takes an hour or so to weed and the side yard less than half of that. The misty rain is light enough that it evaporates off Naomi about as fast as it lands. The work is a black hole for her thoughts — taking them all in and allowing nothing to escape. Soon, the uncertain night before and the knowledge of the boxes in the basement are lost in the plucking and chucking of weeds; a pattern repeated with the use of her hands and not her mind.

Naomi's hair is covered in a bandana to pull the strands from her face and neck. It's a practice that Grandma Dottie utilized. She once claimed in a whispered voice that it kept bad thoughts away. It's a lesson that Naomi carries with her always, even though she mostly covers her hair to keep her curls away from her face. When she was younger, Grandma Dottie had all the magic of a grandma in a movie — silver hair and a satchel of pawpaw fruit.

She held many secrets that she passed to Naomi when her father was in other rooms. She told her that butterflies were visiting spirits, owls signal death, and the pawpaw tree offers protection. There were others, but those memories are mumbled voices and kind eyes now. Memories long repressed by religious aversion and self-preservation. Occasionally, Naomi looks to the pawpaw tree by the garden and wonders why it never protected her or her mama or her Grandma Dottie. But it continues to bear fruit, so she supposes it does still have some use.

Even with her knees covered in dirt and sweat on her brow, Naomi counts herself lucky for the freedom she has.

In her youth, when she was under lock and key, she was seen as a responsible young girl with a good head on her shoulders. She did quite well in class, with few interruptions. Her teachers often remarked that she was eager to please them by assisting in putting away chairs or staying late after class to organize the supplies.

Naomi had a few friends that she played with on the playground.

She was allowed to race around the schoolyard during the day or in the lot by the church in the evenings after her schoolwork was finished. But Eddie Darby refused to allow other children into their home, claiming he was too busy to watch them and didn't want to overwhelm his wife. Naomi was not permitted to spend the night at the houses of the other children either.

This caused a rift early on in her friendships which never truly healed. Enjoying midnight pillow talk about who was cute or the evils of a teacher with your peers in the dim light of the television was an important milestone that Naomi never saw. Not even in her own home.

These wounds were confusing and difficult to heal. Memories intermingle with longing and hope and rage. Freedom came and it wasn't what Naomi thought it would be. It was as though she would be held hostage in the church for her entire life by a man that everyone loved. All of her possible safety nets were a part of his flock and begged *him* for salvation.

How, she had always wondered, *could the Devil bring you salvation? He is the false prophet you fear. A wolf in sheep's clothing. Better yet, a wolf disguised as the shepherd.*

So, Naomi's hate grew. It settled in her gut like mud in a still lake. Sometimes she can see clear through the top few inches of water. She can dip her hand in and witness the beam refract through the liquid as her fingers disrupt the prism of light. As her hand goes deeper, visibility becomes foggier, and the water colder. Soon comes the creeping sensation that something is in the water: a fish too large to swim from, a snapping turtle that will bite her fingers clean off, or a monster that crawls along the bottom waiting for someone who thinks they can risk the murky unknown.

Naomi's hate is always there no matter how clear the surface is.

And how could she escape it? When she can no longer stand to eat grits because she knows how terribly they sting her knees. Each evening at supper, her father would stand over them like God himself. He would hike up her skirt or pull down Aaron's pants so that their bare knees would touch the wood floor of the dining room before they were allowed to pray.

"You must touch the hard ground as Jesus did 'fore you speak to God. He must know you're serious for you to be taken seriously. Or else you're a bug talkin' to the hawk."

I wouldn't mind if I was a bug, Naomi thinks to herself with her hands in the dirt, bringing her focus back to her hands instead of her memories.

As horrible of a gardener as Naomi is, she finds enjoyment in yard work. The artistry and science of it are a bit baffling, but the muscle-memory labor is a drug unto itself. Tasks that engulf a person in repetition have always been of interest to Naomi. At the grocery store, it was bagging at checkout or stocking the shelves. Placing can after can of soup on the metal ledge or gently situating vegetables in a constant stream of plastic grocery bags.

At Davis's, it was collecting crickets to put in to-go buckets or scooping wormy mud into Styrofoam bowls. It was tracing the profile of the river for trash on the canoe to start and end the day.

There's no fervor in this flow. The loss of herself in the task isn't rooted in passion or spark. Just pattern for the sake of peace. The ability to not exist and let her thoughts slip away for however long they might. However long she can keep them away.

A sharp *ding* sounds from the gravel lot on the other side of the house. Naomi's head whips around but she sees nothing. The misty air is still and the soft tapping of rain on the house and trees can be heard all around. She slowly stands and strips off her gardener's gloves.

Her steps are slow and soft on the wet grass, bare feet padding on the saturated earth. The rustling of rocks can be heard before another *ding*. Naomi cautiously peers around the corner to see Clara in a blue raincoat perched on a silver bike. Her bright eyes gaze up at the house as she works to get her kickstand to stick into the gravel.

"Hello," Naomi says, suddenly very self-conscious about the mud that clings to her knees and between her toes. The kind of grime that seems to work its way under her fingernails despite the use of gloves. She's a wet rag compared to Clara, who — even in the rain — glows so brightly that Naomi thinks the water might evaporate right off her.

"Hi, so sorry to surprise you. I meant to give you a few things from the garden yesterday, but it slipped my mind." Clara is still stuck next to her bicycle, which refuses to stand upright. Her fingers tap on the handlebars and her feet continue to fiddle with the kickstand as the rocks part too far to be supportive.

"Here, I got it." Naomi walks barefoot over the rocks to Clara. She hoists the bike over her right shoulder to ascend the front steps and rests it against the wall beside her rocking chair. Clara follows and grabs the plastic bag of tomatoes, basil, and mint from the woven basket perched behind the handlebars.

"Thank you very much. Here." Clara extends the bag to her host. "For yesterday."

"I almost hit y'all," Naomi states bluntly.

"For hanging out. It was nice," Clara smiles. "Are you gardening now?" She glances at Naomi's feet — bare except for the wet earth.

"No. Just pullin' weeds."

"You want some help?"

Long after the morning ends, the pair remain knelt in the yard and pull weeds under the rain. Before they got started, Clara had asked to use the bathroom and sent

Naomi into a worry over what the woman thought of her house. Her cheeks heated up at the possibility she'd left something embarrassing out.

When Clara emerged through the backdoor, though, her raincoat missing and her lovely, freckled shoulders peeking out of her sundress, Naomi quickly replaced her worry with dreams of placing a line of kisses from one shoulder to the other. One for every freckle.

As the day goes on, pauses in their task become regular from the women taking more time to speak than work. Naomi tells her that she was born and raised in Blaire but tries to spend most of her time out of the town's eye. Clara trades this personal information for her own. She and Ethan are both from Kansas City, but Ethan desperately wanted to live in the country, so they compromised. They went rural for Ethan and stayed in Missouri for Clara.

Their friendship comes easy. All four hands are speckled with dirt and their words are sweet. Eventually, they finish their task but the desire for companionship continues to stir between them.

"Is that the garden you were talking about?" Clara points to the worn fence. Naomi describes the garden as it once had been under Grandma Dottie's care: splendid and full of life. The tomatoes were in this corner, the cucumber trellis over there, and herbs grew in that box. Naomi's memory glimmers in the light of how it was and how she wishes she could make it.

"We can do that," Clara says. "We can clear it this fall, replace any wood that's rotted, paint it. Start seeds in late February."

"Ain't that early?" Naomi questions. The troubling thought of *I won't be here then* stumbles through her mind, but she boots it out just as quickly.

"You'd just start them inside. Wait until after the last frost to plant them in the beds." Clara walks through the small entryway into the garden. Thin windy twigs tangle around her legs but she pushes through unafraid of scratches or spiderwebs. She holds her hand out to disrupt the webs before they latch to her as she bends forward to pluck a dandelion.

"We could collect 'em, you know? Make dandelion wine."

Clara twirls the floral weed between her fingers. "You can do that? That's kinda nice. Taking something everybody hates and doing something good with it." She hands the dandelion to Naomi and continues. "What would you like to grow?"

Naomi pauses. She'd planned on replicating Grandma Dottie's garden plan. Not out of loyalty but because she didn't know what else she could do. "I don't know."

"We could try to grow things that'll come back the year after. Every fall and spring you'd do maintenance, but you wouldn't have to replant. Might make it a bit more manageable." They begin to trek to the front porch.

"Manageable is good."

Clara smiles back. It's a slip of sun on an overcast day.

Chapter Nine

The warm and humid days continue well into fall. The air holds more moisture, the morning fogs are thicker. Each morning is chilly but heats up by midday. In a few weeks, the leaves will start to yellow.

The two women become inseparable quickly. Between Naomi's recent unemployment and Clara's time spent as a homemaker, the two find themselves calling on one another nearly every day. She had always looked down on housewives. The job reminded her of her mama and how lousy she was at the mothering part of her duties. She figures that Clara's good at it all, though. So, whether they are eating at Clara's or working in Naomi's garden or making dandelion wine, they are tied at the hip. Naomi is no longer in a rush for her truck to be fixed. If Ethan says it will be a bit longer than expected, then so be it.

After two weeks of chatting and gardening, Naomi calls on Clara to fulfill her part of their deal. The two don swimsuits and carry a cooler and a life jacket to the Kemiwe. Naomi plays tour guide for Clara as she shows her the hidden beaver dams and the red-eared sliders perched on logs to warm their shells. She teaches her about the local wildlife: that the snakes that float are the dangerous ones, and that toes look like food to the catfish that hide in holes in the rocky cliffs lining the bank. Beers are cracked and the canoe is left to bathe in the sun.

Clara's first lesson is to learn to float on her back.

"I thought I was learning to swim today?" Clara asks cheekily.

"You are," Naomi tells her. "But to swim, you gotta float. It's 'bout knowin' how to breathe to keep yourself up. Then, if you ever get tired, you can just get on your back 'n relax. Know you're alright."

The practice includes much splashing as Clara hesitantly learns to trust the water, Naomi, and herself. Her confidence in the task is frail like shale underfoot.

Clara lays on her back with her hair like a halo in the teal water. Naomi's steady hands splay across her back, careful not to budge the straps that hold up her swimsuit. Clara stops her fingers from tearing at Naomi in a desperate attempt to keep herself afloat. Naomi wishes Clara wouldn't stop herself. That Clara would hold on to her for dear life.

This is enough, Naomi chastises herself, *this is intimate enough.*

The comfort that wraps around the two new friends like an old quilt rouses thoughts of Erica again. Naomi never mentioned it to the older woman while she was alive, but later in their friendship, it began to be more akin to that of a mother and her daughter or childhood best friends. Erica talked about her experiences with men and women and life.

She pointed out handsome boys that came through the store to Naomi. Occasionally going as far as closing her aisle to send them to Naomi's.

But the quiet, knobby girl never did have an interest in boys. The entire affair held the sting of every hand raised to her mama or the hands that might have been raised to her brother now that she was no longer there. The thought scared her too much to continue on that path. There was also the other side of that disinterest in boys: the stolen glances at the grace of a woman's fingers, or the curve of a feminine hip. But back then, those thoughts were interrupted by the rattle of Erica's old sedan engine as she drove Naomi home each night.

When the two would sit in the car with windows down in the porch light of Naomi's house, her wide brown eyes would watch Erica's fingers with those long colorful nails roll a joint or two. Blurred tattoos marked her fingers with the ghosts of what were once lightning bolts and stars. The careful process of pressing and tucking fine paper is engraved in her memory as definitively as riding a bike or telling time.

On a particularly rough day after they smoked together, Erica held a joint out for Naomi to take. "For sleep," she said, and squished her nose into a smile.

Those regular trips went on for about a year and a half. Erica never made Naomi pay. She said her time would come to supply, as is the communal nature of sharing weed. Naomi has been buying her own weed for nearly nine years now, ever since Erica died, but she wonders if maybe that time has finally come. She has spent every day for weeks with Clara fulfilling their ends of the initial bargain.

I'll ask her later, Naomi tells herself.

Over time, Naomi's guidance persuades Clara to relax into the river's thrum. Every so often, she takes a short break where she stands beside Naomi. They keep still long enough that life in the water moves past the disruption of humans and fish begin to swim around them, occasionally pecking at their shins.

It's a quiet day. Not a single fisherman or floater has passed by them in hours. It gives the illusion that the river — the entire Ozarks — is their own private swimming hole. Naomi tells Clara any trivia from the area that comes to mind. Her speech isn't rushed or forced or loud. It fills the small space between them with ease.

"When you lie back this time, keep your ears in the water 'n listen for a kinda frog-like sound." Naomi places her calloused fingers on Clara's mid-back until the woman is floating. For the first time, she pulls her hand away and watches her companion stay afloat with her eyes closed. She too lies back in the chilled water.

A pang of guilt echoes in her chest that she pushed for swimming lessons this far into September. It's colder than she prefers for herself.

The familiar gurgling *ribbits* of the catfish nearby bring her back to the river. To Clara. Naomi tunes into the two creatures speaking back and forth somewhere in the river's depths. One is closer, louder than the other.

Naomi explains to her companion how big the freshwater slug-like creatures can get, though they don't grow to their potential in the Kemiwe. That they get bigger in deeper water with more places to hide. She tells Clara that they will eat anything you gave them — like pigs. How Lynn Lake, up by Mountain Springs, hosts an annual noodling competition every June. She tells her that the fish croak from distress and to ward off predators.

For hours, the two women float side-by-side in the cold water, golden chestnut and black, swirling together in the deep azure.

As the sun sets on their day, the cicadas, tree frogs, and crickets begin their chirpings. They buzz along the shore slowly. A fish jumps from the water. A heron flies when the boat draws too close. An otter slides off a fallen tree and into the river.

The women rest in the sunset's glow with sunburns on their noses and beer in their bellies. Arms sore from paddling and fingers puckered from being in the water too long. Clara has packed sandwiches on homemade bread, smeared with fancy mustard and thinly sliced turkey. A soaked lifejacket straddles the front of the canoe. Its torso flaps are left open to dry in the last of the day's light. Clara is bundled in a sweater that envelopes her from shoulder to knee while she drapes her foot over the edge and into the water.

Clara hugs her knee to her cheek and lets her eyes ghost along the tree-lined shore. Naomi wonders which part of the scenery her companion is most interested in. Is it the fish, the heron, the turtle? Maybe it's the shimmer of light on the water. Or the orangey hue that dips into the blue watercolor of the west. Then, the sun falls behind the tree line and Naomi guesses what might really have captured Clara's attention.

The inky emerald of the trees intersects the starry sky, and speckling the darkness is the infinite glittering of lightning bugs.

Although their lights are too frail to illuminate the water or even the faces of the women in the boat, Naomi wants to know what Clara's face looks like in such a light. Something so similar to candlelight on a restaurant tabletop. Even in the dark of night, Naomi still thinks Clara blazes like a fallen firefly. Like she might float up and fly among them.

It's been years since Naomi felt the swell of interest for a woman. Since Erica, it's been only 1990s films with their cropped hair and blue eyeshadow, and the lonely company of her hand. The salacious thought makes her shutter and a spark of guilt lights her belly on fire. A foot ahead of her sits the first companion she has made since Erica. Yet, Naomi is set to repeat the mistake she made with her old friend. Except now, she's making heart eyes at a married woman.

As long as I'm here, I'll never be with her. Or anyone.

"Where are they going?" Clara interrupts Naomi's self-loathing.

One by one, a hundred thousand lightning bugs become a thousand, then only a hundred. As if each has been snuffed out like candles until only two remain. The sparks are only inches apart, tucked in the woods behind Clara, unblinking.

"Where did they go?" Clara's voice is like thunder in the newly fallen silence. *When'd the crickets stop?* That eerie quiet Naomi has felt twice before settles on the water like a heavy fog. Those two lights shine through the forest grow brighter and greener and they get lower and lower.

"I don't know." Naomi grabs her oar and begins to paddle. She's waited in the stillness before, and she won't make that mistake again. Clara follows suit after Naomi, and they row in time. Naomi's chest and head hurt from the heavy kicking of her heart as she tries to get Clara to safety.

Naomi glances over Clara's head, which now glints an unusual silver from the reflection of the moonlight. She sees a pale leg, illuminated by the moon, with skin sagging and wrinkled, extending from the forest shrubbery far below the duo of green orbs.

Naomi quickly looks back at Clara and rows away as fast as the old wooden canoe will let her.

Chapter Ten

The aroma of garlic, onion, and basil fills Naomi's kitchen as she carefully observes Clara's lasagna recipe firsthand. Her freckled fingers delicately pluck basil leaves from the stem before slicing them thinly for garnish. Clara knows the recipe by heart — each ingredient and measurement committed to memory like it really means something. Before Clara leaves, she wishes Naomi luck and gives her a hard copy of the recipe.

Clara's generosity makes Naomi's heart ache in a way that makes her hungry for more. It's a much more pleasant ache than what is crawling up from her gut at the thought of Aaron visiting. Naomi remembers how her mind went numb at the first bite of lasagna several weeks ago. Her thought is that maybe tasting the greatest food that's ever graced her tastebuds might make for a good start to this difficult conversation.

Naomi has stewed in her embarrassment and self-loathing since her previous call with Aaron. It wasn't until she was confronted with a few short hours before facing him again that she realized how unfriendly she had been.

And so soon after his father's funeral.

She likes the sound of *his father's* rather than *our father's.*

Clara was thrilled when Naomi asked if she would be willing to share the recipe. She was even more excited at the prospect of a family reunion. If that's what this dinner could be called. The weight of the years separated weigh Naomi down like lead boots. Years of hoping their relationship might rekindle. And maybe it finally will. Grandma Dottie's wooden box sits on the kitchen counter where Naomi and Aaron would eat dinner.

Naomi's nerves whisper stories of failure in her ear. Her failure to keep her family together. Failure to keep herself safe. Further failures that might come to pass tonight. Her nerves tell her that the table must be set before Aaron arrives so that he knows she has put enough thought into the dinner. She places two plates with two silver forks side-by-side with the steaming lasagna between them.

There has been another aspect of her conversation with Aaron that her mind stumbles back to: "My ol' lady…" Her brother had married, and Naomi never knew. It doesn't puzzle her that she wasn't invited. Even if she were, she wouldn't have gone. She wouldn't have been wanted. However, it was a colossal milestone in his life. In her *little brother's* life. And Naomi missed it. More than missed it.

I didn't even know, she thinks guiltily. *I'd at least got 'em a gift.*

The unmistakable crunch of tires on her drive disrupts her runaway thoughts. A plume of gray dust trails after her father's old sedan — *Aaron's*, she reminds herself. He hops out and tucks his keys into his front pocket before ascending the stairs two at a time.

Naomi propped the front door open fifteen minutes before he was set to arrive. It feels staged. She supposes it is staged, but she hopes it also appears inviting. Her breath catches in her lungs, and she curses herself for not smoking beforehand. But he hasn't spoken to her much since she became a stoner. *What if he can tell the difference?* The panic threatens to geyser from her throat.

"Hello?" Aaron calls from the porch. His knuckles rap on the wooden frame of the screen door.

Naomi clears her throat. "Come on in!" The door screeches, and she curses herself for not oiling the damn thing. "In the kitchen."

Aaron rounds the corner into the kitchen and his smile instantly brightens the room. "I hardly remember my way around this ol' place!" His smile is broad and the geyser inside of Naomi loses some of its force inside her. "It's been a few years. Good to see it again," Aaron adds. "And in such good shape if I may say so, Naomi!"

She blushes at the compliment — at really being seen by him after all this time. The house is the product of years of hard work. She can only imagine the sweat that Grandma Dottie and even Grandpa Richard — when he was still alive — had put into the farmhouse before she did even more on it. To receive any validation that it was worth it is rewarding in itself.

"I added a few layers of paint." The corner of her lips pulls up a bit and she can't quite look her brother in the eye.

"You worker bee! You've been fightin' this place tooth 'n nail, haven't you?" He throws his head back and laughs heartily. Naomi's spirits soar and all of the day's worry is silly in the light of that laugh.

"A bit. She's awfully old," Naomi jokes back.

Aaron removes his black glasses to wipe the tears from his eyes. He sets them back on his nose and claps his hands together in a thunderous beat. "So, what do we have here, sister?"

"Well, I figured I oughta feed you while we do this. It's sausage lasagna. It's got a lot of basil," she speaks quieter than before. "Hope that's alright."

Aaron gestures with his hands to the barstool in front of him. Naomi nods for him to sit. She claims the other stool and pulls a few paper towels for the two of them. Aaron sits still and admires the dish. "This looks lovely! Why don't you serve, sister."

With a square on each plate, Naomi digs in but pauses when she notices that Aaron's head is bowed in prayer. Her fork pauses only a moment. *This is my house. I don't have to pray if I don't wanna. This is my house*, Naomi repeats to herself. However, she waits to take her next bite until he finishes.

Barely allowing himself time to swallow before speaking, Aaron praises the dish. "Lily would love this recipe. You mind sharin'?" The man scoops a second helping onto his plate. Naomi's chest swells with pride.

"Remind me to write it down 'fore you leave," Naomi asks.

With her own — much smaller — portion of lasagna finished, Naomi's attention returns to the box. Its brown stain looks horribly out of place against the pale countertops. Like it's been plucked from the past and dropped there, even after having been wiped with a rag to remove the decades of dust that accumulated.

"Now, 'fore we get into this, we both gotta wash our hands. These pictures — the notes 'n books — are old 'n we ain't about to get our grubby, greasy hands all over 'em," Naomi tries to use a tone that conveys how serious she is without being rude.

Aaron wipes his mouth with the paper towel. "Yes, ma'am." He washes his hands vigorously. When their hands are dried and the leftover lasagna is stowed in the fridge, Naomi sets the small trunk between them.

"Between each picture, there're notes, so we gotta make sure we keep it all in order." She unlatches it carefully.

With the hands of a gentle giant, Aaron reaches within and pulls out the same stack she looked through her first time with the collection. Naomi studies him carefully. His lips are pulled upward as he gazes upon his big sister as a small, curly-headed tot and his Grandma Dottie. He reads the note attached, then pauses. Aaron places a new paper towel down on the counter before setting the photo on top, the picture down. Naomi's heart sings because of how carefully he handles their family treasures.

The next picture is him with his naked chest and overalls. Aaron's eyes well up with tears. "Naomi," he sputters. "I hardly remember her." He rakes his hand over his mouth before removing his glasses and pressing the heel of his hand deep into his eyes.

It's an experience that Naomi knows bitterly. The realization of how much was kept from them. How little they know about a family that hasn't moved from the same spot on the map in nearly two hundred years. All that time their kin lived here, and yet there is so little known about the people even just two generations back. Naomi watches her brother realize how quickly a person can vanish from family history.

Naomi scratches at the skin around her fingernails as Aaron continues to flip through the photos until he reaches the bottom. Ever so attentively, he places them back and closes the lid.

"You found quite the treasure, Naomi." His voice is mellower than it was when he first arrived. His presence is more comfortable resting beside her. Her hands relax and her chest no longer aches.

"There's more but I haven't gone through 'em yet," she admits. The other two boxes still wait in the dark and dirty cellar. Guilt builds in her chest again at the thought.

A warm hand rests over her own. "I can't wait to see what you find." And neither can she. "It's a pity what she became."

And the illusion breaks.

"What?" Naomi sputters.

"That Grandma Dottie left God after Mama had you," Aaron responds as if Naomi should have known the whole time.

"Aaron, you saw the photos — the notes. Grandma Dottie loved Mama. She loved us." *Who gives a damn?* Naomi wants to scream at him.

He sighs deeply. "I see what you mean. It's just—" he pauses. "It's hard to feel like that — like I think you want me to feel — for somebody I don't know." Aaron takes a deep breath before he begins again. "Maybe I can stop by again? Give you some time to look through the rest. How 'bout the second Wednesday in October? Is a week and a half enough?

As frustrated as Naomi is, she understands. Although she doesn't see Grandma Dottie in that light — *especially* after looking through the photos that were collected with such adoration, annotated with such *love* — she does feel that way about their father. There has always been a wall between them. Naomi knows that it makes sense that Aaron feels the same way about a woman they saw maybe once or twice a year. Not to mention that Grandma Dottie died when Aaron was only six and Naomi nine.

Those three years, it seems, made a difference.

"It's alright," Naomi offers comfort to her brother. She wishes she could pry herself open and empathize with the man. *I can't bring myself to care much for Father*, she imagines herself telling Aaron. *So, I get it, little brother.* "It's alright."

Chapter Eleven

As Clara's garden begins to yellow with the approaching harvest season, and a sprinkling of bronze leaves litter her yard, the two women increase their time spent in the garden. She keeps a small fold-out stool near the open gate of her garden for workdays. However, Naomi opts to settle into a childlike pose with her knees nearly touching her ears and feet planted firmly on the ground. They each cradle a wooden basket close to overflowing with fruits and vegetables and herbs.

Clara often speaks, a toothpick wedged between her lips, of what she plans to plant next year when the garden can fully be her own. When there's time to start her seeds indoors rather than fertilize whatever old Tim Willis planted however many years ago. She has a child's pencil box full of labeled bags of seeds that she collected from her garden in Kansas City. She promises some to Naomi.

Clara prances over to greet Ethan when he emerges from the house. They are too distant to hear but Clara's eyebrows pull together and her nose scrunches up. Ethan's face remains cool and detached, hands on his hips. Naomi doesn't want to stare, but Ethan catches her and shoots a glare her way before she can glance away. She busies herself with the rosemary at her feet.

"Everythin' alright?" Naomi questions upon Clara's return.

Clara moves her hands through the bushes in such a confident manner it's hard to imagine the woman has difficulty doing anything. As if she can conduct all of the life in her garden like an orchestra. "I think he's used to having me all to himself. He just misses me is all."

So much of Naomi and Clara's time in the past few weeks has been spent together. During that time, Ethan is usually working — either in his garage or off wherever with his marshal duties — and the pair are only at Clara's home a third of the time they spend together. During the rest, they are either at Naomi's or exploring the hills and hollers of Ozark country.

The last thing Naomi wants is to overstay her welcome in Clara's life. "Should I give y'all some space?"

Clara stops. Her fingers are suddenly unsure of their next move. "No. He'll be alright."

"Will you?"

"Definitely," and she smiles that peachy grin and gets back to work.

Their list of garden tasks wanes and a bottle of wine is eventually opened. They lounge on patio furniture with their half-full glasses. Naomi imagines them as a part of a scene in a movie or a department store ad. After two, Clara fishes a toothpick from behind her ear and becomes particularly chatty.

She explains that she and Ethan met out of high school — when *she* was fresh out of high school. Clara was nineteen and Ethan was twenty-eight. She was living outside of the city in Independence in an effort to avoid the higher rent of Kansas City. The suburban house was shared by two other girls from her job at a local burger joint. The trio went to a house party one spring and quickly fanned out among the other partygoers. Clara found herself uncomfortable and in need of somewhere quiet which led her outside for a smoke.

When Clara mentioned the word, she gripped the toothpick between her teeth a little tighter. Ethan was huddled under the small awning that protected them from a spring shower, a cigarette in hand. They chatted and left the party together. Their relationship happened nearly all at once. One day they met, and for the next however many, they woke up together.

It sparks something in Naomi's imagination. If Ethan weren't in the picture, would things be different between her and Clara? Would Naomi be able to charm her the same way? The film in her head projects a story of Naomi still teaching Clara to swim, and Clara returning the favor with gardening lessons.

However, in her version of the story, there are far more stolen glances between them. Their fingers meet in the dirt and their breaths catch. The cool water enchants Clara to cuddle close to Naomi as the sun begins to fall. Their thighs hold one another when Naomi grows the balls to kiss her. Not a stolen kiss, but one where Clara draws herself closer and glances up from Naomi's lips to tell her *I want this, too. I want you, too.*

But Clara keeps talking about Ethan, and Naomi lets the fantasy slip away like smoke in the wind. Clara spills into another tale from years ago, when Ethan fell off a dock into February waters while they were sledding. She tells stories in a way that is passionately engaging and chronologically nightmarish. Everything she says holds value emotionally but not necessarily to the plot. Her hands — which are so precise while gardening — wave around her like she's flagging down a train. One of these gestures is too sharp and blood-red wine sloshes from the glass in her hand and spills onto the stone patio.

"Woah there, doll. I think you've had enough." Ethan scoops the wine glass from Clara's extended palm, interrupting the story. He was present long enough to have a wrinkle between his eyes that makes Naomi believe he's either angry or embarrassed by the story she's telling.

"I'm not drunk. You remember that time we went sledding by that pond?" Clara's feet are splayed over the armrest, lavender toenails chipped with summer use.

"Nope, sorry. Now, hun, why don't you head inside? I'll clean your plate." Ethan collects the glasses from the iron patio table.

"Ethan, the one you fell in!" Clara rolls her eyes with a smile on her face and turns to Naomi. "He swore up and down the ice was thick, and sure enough, he wasn't on there for two seconds and there was this loud *crack!* and a big splash. I was over on the dock — it was kinda hard to tell the dock from the water, but the water was a few inches lower so you could kinda tell that way — and I had to run over and—"

Ethan turns and leaves. His irritation seeps into the atmosphere like toxic gas. Clara trails off her story to some lackluster conclusion. Naomi's eyes follow Ethan, and she spies him cleaning their drinkware through the kitchen window. His brows are still pinched together, his mouth a flat line. *What's up his ass?*

"I'm gonna run inside real quick." Clara springs up.

Naomi decides it might be an opportune time to start to leave. Midwestern goodbyes are a notoriously long process. She follows after Clara a few minutes later but slows as she overhears aggravated whispering from the living room. Naomi pauses behind a wall, out of sight of the couple.

She hears Ethan telling Clara that she's acting foolish and drunk. That he's worried about her, he *always* worries about her. Drinking isn't healthy. That it turns Clara into someone he doesn't know. It turns him off. These are intermingled with *I love you, baby*, *I'm not mad just disappointed*, and *maybe we should have some alone time*.

Naomi's used to ignoring what people — particularly the men of Blaire — want from her. Even at a woman's quietest, her presence, her *existence*, is often too loud for small men. And Ethan is showing himself to be just that. The way he uses his words to squeeze around Clara's resilience like a boa with a deer. It reminds Naomi too much of her father. And what he did with his open palm was perpetuated by his tongue. It's hard for her to remember which one stung more.

Naomi takes a few silent steps back before retracing her steps much louder back to where the living room meets the kitchen.

"Hey, Clara. I was thinkin' — ope, sorry. Didn't mean to interrupt." She does. Clara's arms are tight across her chest. Ethan sits on the couch looking fed up. Naomi's not sure if he's more done with her or Clara.

"It's okay. Actually, Ethan wanted to let you know that your truck is done!" Clara plasters on a plastic smile.

Oh shit. Have three weeks really gone by so fast? It's a novel experience, not wanting to leave. Suddenly, it's as if a snow globe full of all her favorite things — the Kemiwe River or her favorite pizza spot in Mountain Springs — has shattered and left her with broken bits to bury. Places she could never go with her family but are now havens discovered in her solitude. Small treasures she seemingly only recently began to hold tight to seem so close to being lost.

And one of those treasures is Clara.

"Thank you, Ethan. I appreciate it."

"Yeah, for sure. Happy to help."

Something must be done. Naomi doesn't want to part from Clara just like that. The house can be sold at any time. The changes are all cosmetic, excuses really.

"I'll walk you out to your car." Clara grabs Naomi's keys off the coffee table and walks up to her. The two make their way out the back door.

The moon is high and lightning bugs and bats dance through the trees. "I guess I'll be leavin' soon then."

It hurts even more once spoken.

"Where to?"

"I'll probably stay at a hotel in Kansas City 'til I find an apartment. Got any suggestions?" She half-heartedly teases.

Inside the garage, the truck is no longer crushed and bent. Patches of deep blue paint are missing on the passenger side which was something Ethan had warned Naomi of. The passenger window is gone, and the windshield is cracked. He had not mentioned that he wouldn't be completing those parts.

"It might be a while 'til we see each other again," Naomi mutters.

"My folks still live in KC. I'll be up there once or twice a year." Clara's light smile is almost convincing.

"You could come over tonight." An embarrassed burn races over Naomi's face and chest. "Like a sleepover." She hears herself in the voice of a gangly, awkward thirteen-year-old. One who doesn't have friends, who doesn't actually know what a sleepover is like outside of movies.

But like another thirteen-year-old, so hopeful for companionship, Clara's eyes light up. She looks back to the house, likely considering Ethan's current emotional state. "I'll text Ethan and let him know. Is it okay if I borrow some of your clothes for tonight?"

Gravel kicks up around their feet as they approach the front door of Naomi's home. Clara points in the direction of the garden. "What the heck is that? I don't think I've ever asked."

Naomi looks up, half expecting to see the *thing* that hasn't shown itself recently. Instead, at the end of Clara's gesture is the pawpaw tree.

Clara wanders off the path towards it. Her bright eyes notice the pea-tinted pods of fruit sprinkled throughout its browning leaves. "And what are those?"

Naomi follows suit and withdraws a pocketknife from her jeans to harvest a fist-sized fruit from its stem. She turns to the woman with the halved sweet. Clara plucks a slice and pops it between her lips. Naomi does the same. They both stand in the darkness with sugary tongues.

"You can take some home if you like," Naomi offers, her thoughts lingering on the fresh produce Clara often sent her home with. "It's a pawpaw tree. They're all over down here."

With Naomi's knife, they cut down a few more ripened pods for Clara to return home with the next day.

Chapter Twelve

In all the years of living in her grandma's house, Naomi has never felt at home. The pictures that once lined the walls were not of people she loved or even knew, with the exception of Grandma Dottie, Grandpa Richard, and her mama. The paint colors on the walls aren't the colors she likes. It's a single-occupancy hotel room she's rented for the last twelve years. Sometimes, especially lately, it's like she may share the place with ghosts.

But Clara sits on the couch with her feet tucked under her. She looks very much at home. The house isn't so strange with her there. It's homey and familiar. Naomi gives her some well-worn pajama pants and an old band t-shirt much too large for her. The shirt was snagged from Erica years before.

By the door, Naomi spies the blue raincoat that Clara forgot on her first visit. If she lets her mind wander, it's almost like Clara stays the night every night. Like each morning they stand, hip to hip, and make breakfast. Like they share showers and shampoo and pillows.

Naomi pulls a joint from her stash jar. Clara says she's smoked weed before, but it's been a while. After a few drags, she confesses that Ethan has a problem with her smoking and drinking and anything of the sort. They stopped smoking cigarettes years before in the interest of their health. Naomi pretends she didn't overhear earlier.

"Drinking isn't healthy. It turns you into somebody I don't know, Clara. Honestly, it's a turn-off." She recalls. Naomi finds herself starkly disagreeing with Ethan as Clara presses lush mauve lips over the filter of the joint. Her cheeks hollow slightly as she inhales, and her eyes flutter closed like she's engaged in a marijuana kiss.

"He gets weird about it. I don't know. I love him, but Jesus can I get five minutes? You know?"

"Well, you can come smoke 'n drink with me whenever." Naomi offers her warmest smile in condolence. "You want somethin' to drink? I don't have any alcohol."

"Yes, please. What do you have?"

"Water, orange juice, and cola." Naomi walks to the kitchen.

"Oh! Cola please!"

Naomi grabs two glass beverages from the fridge and briefly scans the shelves for something to make for dinner. She tries to be frugal, but cold, glass colas are a weakness of hers. So much of her money goes to fixing the house or saving for her move. Colas and cannabis are the two luxuries she regularly allows herself.

Fireflies flicker outside by the garden. It's common to spot critters in her backyard wilderness, and there always seems to be something making a home in the garden.

Despite its unruliness, she supposes it's a perfect habitat for the bugs and animals to enjoy. The sweet fruits of the pawpaw tree also attract a few butterflies here and there, too.

Naomi cracks open the drinks but the trace of a shadow in the backyard makes her freeze. She drops the glass cola and it shatters on the floor, glass and fizzy drink spreading over the hardwood like the bloom of blood from a gunshot. Clara is at her side immediately. She clasps Naomi's hands between her own, calloused on the tips of her fingers and pads of her palms, searching for blood. Her fingers track up her arms and to her face, so close to Naomi's face.

"What happened? Did any of it get you?" The concern in her voice makes Naomi's heart flutter.

"No, I'm alright," Naomi falsely promises.

"Can you grab me some paper towels? Maybe something to spray so it doesn't get sticky?" Clara asks.

Naomi's eyes remain locked on the dining window as she retrieves the items for her friend. The darkness on the outside doesn't falter. It's a steady sheet of blackness. Clara begins to collect pieces of glass and chuck them into the trash.

"Man, I haven't had one in a long time!" Clara calls as she cleans.

"Mhmm." Taking advantage of the privacy, Naomi creeps closer to the kitchen window.

The shadow could have been from a hundred things: bear, deer, mountain lion, raccoon. Hell, even wild horses are a possibility.

However, there is another possibility. One she prays isn't there. One she tries so hard not to let Clara know about. Naomi's nose is nearly pressed against the cool glass.

"I don't mean to pry, but do you happen to have any more bottles?" Clara asked.

The half-moon ignites the treetops in a cool glow and reflects off the dew in the grass. Even with her hands cupped around her eyes to shield from the houselights, Naomi sees nothing. No deer, no bears. Just a dark, empty yard leading up to a dark, empty forest.

Until a speck of movement draws her eyes up.

Two corpse-like feet begin to descend from the top of the window. They are nearly translucent in the moonlight. Like its guts would be visible through the pale, thin skin of its stomach. Like she would be able to see the blood pumping through its blue veins.

Naomi snatches the blinds closed.

"Naomi?"

She spins around. Clara stands in the kitchen. The floor is clean of sticky soda and glass. "I asked if you have any more?"

"Uh yeah, I should." Naomi opens the fridge and points to the remaining two bottles. There's a rap at the dining room window. Like acrylic nails on a tabletop. They both twist around to face it. Naomi's heart is a block of ice. Clara takes a step to approach it, but her friend's hand wraps around her wrist.

"It's just a stick in the gutter. It's alright," Naomi tries to assure her, but she is positive that Clara can feel her wild pulse through her palm. Or at least her furious sweating.

Then, there's another rap on the glass of the back door.

Then, a knock at the front door.

"What the fuck is that?" Clara shakes Naomi's hand from her wrist and takes a step toward the living room.

Naomi struggles to speak. Like the feet are crammed down her gullet. "It could be raccoons." Her excuse is sour.

"Are you expecting someone?"

"You're about the only visitor I've had in a long time," Naomi admits. Then another knock. Clara takes a few steps toward the door. "Clara, don't."

"Okay." The door handle shakes. "Oh shit," Clara whispers.

Naomi pulls the rest of the curtains closed. When she turns back, Clara is calling 911.

"Wait—"

"911, where is your emergency?" Naomi can hear the operator from a few feet away. Naomi doesn't want to call the authorities. Ethan isn't welcome in her house. Especially not tonight. Even if it is an emergency, she would rather handle it herself than deal with the marshal.

Fuck. Maybe I oughta bought that dog like Grandma Joyce said.

Clara tells the operator the basic information: the address, the person trying to get in, and that her husband is the marshal. Amid her hushed description, there are a series of taps on the kitchen window, then in the living room, and the dining area. The front door handle still jiggles and the hair on Naomi's neck stands on end. The curtains that cover all the windows might as well be transparent with how exposed she is.

Clara was never supposed to know about this. It was supposed to go away.

Naomi grabs the phone from Clara and puts it on the coffee table.

"Clara, that ain't gonna help." Naomi pauses. She looks into Clara's amber eyes, and she wants so badly for her friend to understand without her having to say it. About the green eyes that keep finding her and the sickly pale legs that float through the forest. It's unbelievable and Naomi knows it, but with every window in the house drumming from a hundred long fingers, it can't just be crazy anymore. Something must be real.

"Clara, somethin's in the woods."

Clara's eyes grow wide as saucers. The terror matches her own but the sincerity in them is what encourages Naomi that she has made the right choice — to say something. However, despite asking the impossible, Clara's confidence in her companion doesn't falter.

"What do we do?" Clara whispers.

"I don't know."

All at once, the tapping stops. The doorknob goes still. The beam of a flashlight streaks through the glass of the front door. The muffled noise of two men talking draws the women to approach. Naomi pulls aside a curtain to peek outside. Marshal Wilder stands on the other side beside Aaron.

As Naomi unlocks and opens the door, Clara steps down to the porch and is rushed by Ethan.

"Babe, I was so worried! You left the house and didn't tell me where you were. You scared me." Ethan wraps his arms around her like a lock, but she doesn't return the gesture. Her eyes frantically sweep the yard looking for an answer to the mysterious tapping. "Then I got a call for this address." Ethan pointedly looks at her. "Naomi."

"Marshal," she matches his neutral tone. Before now, it was easy to forget he's replaced one of her father's roles in the community. However, now he's on her doorstep with a ten-gallon hat and a badge. Naomi follows Clara's gaze over the yard and then up to the trees, looking for any sign of the creature.

"Ethan, I did text you. I told you where I was and what I was doing." Her response is punctuated with anger. "And the call—"

"But babe—" he cuts her off. "You guys were drinking. You shouldn't be driving." He holds his hands around her upper arms. It makes her look smaller than Naomi ever wants to see her.

"Is that right?" Aaron finally speaks up.

"You gotta be shittin' me," Naomi laughs. "Aaron, what are you even doing here?"

"We said we'd meet on Wednesday. I didn't think to call ahead," Aaron says sheepishly. "Naomi, were you drinkin' and drivin'?"

"I was drinking. Naomi had less than half a glass." Clara is quick to defend her friend.

"I'll take a breathalyzer if we can be done with it." Naomi stands her ground. "I haven't looked through the rest, Aaron. It'll have to be another time."

"You know it smells a little skunky around here, too, Darby." Ethan takes a step toward the door trying to peek inside.

Fuck, I left the jar and joint out. Naomi steps outside and closes the door behind her. "Yeah, we're in the woods. There're skunks sometimes," Naomi tries to redirect his attention. "Wilder, you got a warrant or somethin'? 'Cus you're sure as hell not invited inside."

The marshal laughed. "What am I? A damn vampire? I'm worried about my girl!"

His girl.

"This is goddamn ridiculous. You wanna sobriety test me or are we done?"

"Well, they got here safe, right? 'Sides, Marshal, cannabis was legalized in the good state of Missouri."

Ethan looks up as if to ask God for assistance. "Safe, Pastor? My wife called about a break-in, and it reeks of weed. There's nothin' I can do about that? I could get DEA out here under the suspicion that you're sellin', Naomi." He pointed his finger at her. "Clara, did you get a good look at him? Was he some sort of dealer?"

You motherfucker, Naomi thought heatedly. She opened her mouth to go off but was interrupted.

"It was a raccoon," Clara says. "I called because I got scared but we watched it run off after it messed with the door a little. I just got paranoid after smoking. That's all. I don't want to go home. You've been up my ass all night. I want to stay with Naomi."

I want to stay with Naomi.

Ethan's eyes nearly bulged out of his skull. "*You* were smoking too?"

Aaron claps a hand on the marshal's back, but the mustached man quickly shakes it off. "Free country, Ethan. Ain't much we can do about legal weed and a nosey raccoon."

Ethan shoots Aaron a nasty look. "You just gonna let 'em walk all over you like that? That ain't how shit's done in my house, but I suppose if your meat don't swing, then you ain't got much else in your corner. Do you?" Ethan looks at the pastor, expecting him to shrivel like a cock in a snowstorm.

Aaron gestures for Ethan to follow him down the stairs. "Come on, marshal. Let's leave the girls be. We can grab a drink at the church and cool off a bit, 'fore we head our separate ways."

With white knuckles latched to his belt, Ethan turns to Naomi. "I better not get any more calls about my wife and you, Darby. No more foul smells, neither."

Clara exaggeratedly sniffs the air. "I don't smell nothin'."

"Me neither," Naomi adds.

The crunch of gravel under tires grows distant as Naomi watches the cars driving single file down the dusty road. It doesn't take much more convincing for Ethan to leave, but eventually, the pseudo-cowboy begrudgingly climbs into that green monstrosity on his way to Blaire Baptist.

Naomi double-checks every door and window, ensuring everything is locked and covered. All the downstairs lights are turned off and the two women climb the stairs to bed.

Naomi isn't sure how to proceed with the sleepover. It's hit what can kindly be called a rough patch, and now she grasps at straws for what to do with sleeping arrangements.

Is sharing a bed alright? The evening was shattered, and she isn't sure it's possible to return to the coziness of before.

Clara throws herself onto the bed, feet dangling off. Her hand rests on her stomach. Naomi closes the heavy wooden door behind her. "Is it alright if I lock it?"

"Lock it as many times as you can." She doesn't look away from the ceiling. "I'm sorry about all of that. I'm so fucking sorry." Clara rubs her eyes roughly. When she withdraws, her mascara is a blurred black line beneath bloodshot eyes.

"It's alright." It isn't. But Naomi wishes she could make it so. Especially when Clara looks so pretty and so distressed. The desire to crawl into bed with her and pepper her in kisses until the name *Ethan* is erased from her mind, washes over her like she's plunged into the Kemiwe.

Clara sits up and pushes herself against the bed's headboard, knees pulled to her chest. "That couldn't have just been him outside, Naomi. Even if your brother was knocking on the windows, too."

Naomi's dream of domesticity and love breaks apart with her words.

Clara continues to press. "It was all around us."

"Mmhmm."

Her companion's back straightens and her knees drop. Golden brown strands cascade down between her shoulder blades. "Did you see anything before they showed up?"

"It was dark," Naomi dismisses. Whatever it is, Clara doesn't need to be involved, Naomi decides at that moment. *She's already dealing with that controlling asshole.* She doesn't need whatever is prowling the woods to give her nightmares, too.

And it's been so long since Naomi has had someone to be close with. She'll be damned if she lets that *thing* drive this beautiful woman out of town and out of sight in Ethan's passenger seat.

Naomi sits down on the edge of the quilted mattress. The door is at her back, but with Clara there she doesn't feel as vulnerable.

"No, you said there's something in the woods." Clara's eyes look too deeply into her own. Naomi doesn't want her friend to see what she has seen. She wants her to be spared the terror she has been exposed to in the past few weeks — spared all the horrors life can have.

However, another part of Naomi screams for her to spill her guts. To share this lonely ghost story with someone. It's a puzzle too difficult for one person alone. She wishes for Clara to collect all of the pieces and hold them gently in her hands to help Naomi assemble them. To make sense of the nonsensical because, so far, on her own, she has solved nothing. She has gained no knowledge; she has come no closer to safety.

I got Clara into this now.

It can no longer be chalked up to a hallucination. Something is lurking in the woods, outside of her house. Naomi can't ignore it any longer, but she also can't let Clara get stuck in this haunted house either. *She can't know.*

"Are there any stories about this kinda thing around here?" Clara asks, like Naomi has a campfire story to tell.

"My folks didn't let talk like that happen at our house. Maybe I just never heard." Naomi curses her father for possibly keeping her in the dark about one more thing.

"Is there anyone we can ask?"

"I'm not sure. I'm not—" Naomi pauses, worried about alienating herself too much in Clara's eyes. She doesn't want to look like a pariah to someone so dear. "I'm not close to folks around here."

Clara is quiet for a while. She pulls on a loose thread from the drawstring of her borrowed pajama pants. "I'm sorry you've been on your own." Then Clara places her hand over Naomi's, and Naomi wishes so badly that this moment could be paused and saved and that the rest of the night could wash away.

Chapter Thirteen

The morning after their sleepover uncovers a raw nerve for Naomi. The worry of what will come to Clara once she gets home — once she's out of Naomi's sight — eats away at her. The pair slept side by side like two lungs. Morning eyes first meet each other's, then the dew on the bedroom windows. The mid-October sunrise is chilly and fog leaks into the yard from the river. Rays of sunlight peek through the lines of the thin tree trunks.

Clara chops the potatoes and Naomi fries them. The kitchen is smokey and messy. Bare toes pad on the wood floors with glasses of orange juice in hand. The domestic act gives her a sense of usefulness. Too often she finds herself at the vulnerable receiving end of Clara's charity. Not having to repeat her gratitude leaves her considerably more comfortable as they sit on the couch eating.

Although Ethan might as well be a damn helicopter, Naomi hasn't *seen* anything reportable or even cruel enough to be able to sit down with Clara and tell her to kick the bastard to the curb. However, she knows she only sees a portion of their relationship — only as much as is made public or as Ethan allows to be seen.

Naomi also knows that no one stepped up about her father either. Surely, folks saw bruised wrists or an occasional limp, but nothing was ever done. Who would question the reverend and marshal in the same breath? Those situations often go unseen, uncared for. They fester in secret like bedsores on the back of a patient. Their hair may be brushed, their nails may be clean, but if someone would just take the time — the care — to flip them to their side and take a proper look, then the rotting hole of neglect — abuse — would be seen.

Yet, Naomi has no proof of either. There's no evidence that Ethan is anywhere near as severe as her father was. It's entirely possible that he could just be an asshole sometimes like damn near everybody else. There isn't much to do about an asshole besides waiting for them to fuck up enough that Clara herself decides to be done with him.

Naomi drops Clara off after their meal. Ethan's waiting on the porch with his elbows on his knees, his expression weary. Dark circles hold his eyes in their violet palms and Naomi can't help but roll her own at his dramatic response. As if Naomi is a terrible influence beyond a little age-appropriate drug use and getting his wife out of the house a few times a week. Clara immediately waves for him to follow her to the front door. He walks past her and inside. Naomi raises her hand through the passenger window to her friend. Clara does the same with a tightlipped smile.

Clara doesn't visit Naomi's home for a few weeks. Her door remains open to Naomi, but Ethan always hovers nearby. He pulls Clara's seat closer to his when they eat dinner. He peeks out of the garage while they collect fall squash before the first frost sets in. He insists on building the fire when Naomi and Clara want to sit under the stars on cold nights even though they don't want the smoke to smudge out the twinkling lights.

His presence makes Naomi increasingly more uncomfortable. Clara tries to play it off but sometimes Naomi hears her talking to Ethan about giving her space.

The next week, Clara sends her a letter telling her that things with Ethan need to cool. That he's hurt by what he perceived as "not enough communication" regarding that night. They're deciding to heal with a little more time together in the near future. In words that to Naomi's ears did not sound her own, Clara claims that after their move to Blaire, the two have been stressed and not caring for their relationship enough. So, Naomi locks herself at home and waits.

Naomi's newfound time alone is filled with housework. Her lonesome mind often meanders to her companion. What she might be doing, what Ethan might be doing, if she should stop by, if Clara will ever stop by again. The handful of isolated weeks start slowly with half-assed attempts from Naomi at completing productive tasks. She finishes cleaning the basement, a large drop-off at a thrift store in Mountain Springs, the pale blue paint for the garden is finally purchased. Time struggles forward like a dog without the use of its hind legs. It hurts and the end destination is futile. Wasted energy is what it often seems like to Naomi.

As Clara's appearances in Naomi's life decrease in frequency, Aaron becomes her prime source of company. His sedan chugs down the drive once or twice a week. In the beginning, he opens his car door with a dish in hand. Lily's cooking rivals Grandma Joyce and Clara's. The two sit on the couch when it's chilly and on the floor in front of the fireplace when it's downright cold.

It's casual. So much so that she grasps at hazy memories of sneaking blackberries from the neighbor's patch when they were kids. Four knees crusted in mud, crouched in the spiky brambles. Their fingers and lips and tongues stained violet.

On their third week of private get-togethers, his driver's side door opens, and his always-black work shoes step out. Then, Naomi spots a bulb of mahogany hair on the other side of the car. It makes its way to the front of the vehicle and Naomi sees the loose bun that sits atop the head of a very short woman. Her wide brown eyes aren't even able to see over the top of the car. She skirts around the hood in her capris and baby blue sweater.

Naomi hasn't spent much time pondering what Lily might look like or be like. She curses herself for it now. How insensitive it was to not give a damn about her brother's wife. The person that's been cooking and baking for her for weeks.

"Hi, nice to meet you, Naomi." Her voice is sweet tea.

"Naomi," Aaron's eyes are bright behind his black-rimmed glasses as his hand lays itself lightly at his wife's lower back. "This is my Lily. It's nice that y'all finally get to meet."

Still feeling like boiled shit for her thoughtlessness, Naomi extends her hand to Lily. "It's nice to meet you. You're cookin's been a joy."

Lily looks at Naomi's hand and shuffles the dish she carries between her hands in an attempt to free one to meet Naomi's greeting. With her second mistake out in the open for all to see, Naomi backtracks with reddened cheeks. Her hands flail as she tries to help.

"Oh sorry. It's alright. Here, lemme—" She takes the dish from Lily and hurries inside. With a dishtowel underneath, she rests it on the counter and perks her head up to see Lily and Aaron speaking in hushed voices on the porch. He leans in and kisses his wife's cheek. Her smile grows brilliantly, as does a sprout of jealousy in Naomi's chest.

"I hope it's alright I sprung this on you, sister." Aaron strips off his charcoal jacket and places it on one of the hooks beside the front door next to Clara's blue raincoat. Naomi's cheeks heat up and she worries he'll see it. That he'll ask questions or, worse yet, that all of Blaire already has notions about what Clara and Naomi have been up to — that *he* might think something.

"S'alright." Her voice a mouse's squeak.

Lily's hands wrap around one another as she speaks. "I baked a coffee cake this time. I hope you like it." Her gaze shifts to her husband and he nods with a smile.

Naomi's on the outs. She knows it. It's all choreographed, rehearsed. "Sure I will."

A quiet lies between them. It keeps them apart. It keeps Naomi from asking any questions that might bring her relief from her fears. She and Aaron haven't sat in tension like this since his first visit. Since then, it has eased like molasses. It's sweet and sticks them together like when they were little.

"See, I told Lily about the photos of us when we were tiny with Grandma Dottie. And the notes—"

"I'm really hopin' I can take a peek," Lily interrupts. "And whenever you get to lookin' at the rest of it, I'd love to see it, too." Aaron's hand latches on to her's and squeezes. Brown doe eyes gaze up at him, but he keeps his hopeful stare on Naomi.

"Course." Naomi's shoulders drop and her back relaxes. Maybe they don't think anything. Maybe the raincoat is hers if they ask about it. Maybe they know she and Clara are just friends. *Just friends.* "Gimme a minute to go fetch 'em."

The trio of boxes rests in their basement cave. Naomi checks that she is retrieving the correct one before she ascends the stairs. Before whispering stops her.

"I'll talk to her, I will, Lily. I promise." Her brother's words send an icy shot of fear through Naomi. Perhaps she jumped the gun assuming he knows nothing.

"I just don't want anything bad—"

"She's my sister. I don't want that neither," Aaron huffs.

Naomi takes each step louder than the last. She's tired of being a ghost. Tired of treading on silent feet that carry her to conversations she wishes she hadn't heard. "Got 'em." She sets the box on the coffee table.

The couple gathers around the treasure chest and ooh-s and ahh-s at each chubby cheek and childhood fact about the baby boy.

Lily insists on cleaning the evening's plates herself. Naomi tries to put up a fight but loses when Aaron asks her to step outside with him. It's an inevitable request. It was foreshadowed not an hour before, but it was easy to forget while Naomi sat in her living room with her *family*. Maybe it's an inevitable end to their newfound relationship, too. *It wasn't made to last,* she thinks bitterly.

Aaron waves his hand toward the rocking chair on the porch and Naomi sits down like a good dog. He rests his hips on the railing and crosses his long legs at the shin. His hands rest, clasped, but relaxed in front of him. "So, the marshal's visit."

"Why've we got to hash this out? Nothin' happened. You heard him even threaten me with fuckin' DEA!" Naomi starts ranting and leans forward in her seat to stand up. Her nervous energy quickly converts into seething anger.

Aaron simply holds his hand up as a signal to stop. And Naomi does. "After so long of you bein' — what I assume — is awful lonely, I'm delighted to hear that you've got a friend." Aaron pauses to look out over the yard toward the garden and the pawpaw tree. "But her *husband* was not pleased, Naomi."

"Oh, to hell with what her husband thinks!" Naomi throws back at him. "Clara's an adult. She can make her own choices."

"Naomi, can you simmer down for a dang minute. I'm tryin' to talk and not get bit." He crosses his arms as if to show that he's done playing around. "Now, Ethan Wilder is our new marshal. I imagine that's a sensitive thing for you, him bein' father's replacement 'n all. He's started comin' to

Sunday service. He's talked to me about how he's feelin' in all of this. The man just wants more time with his wife! Ain't nothin' wrong with that."

Naomi is already exhausted from the conversation. "What's all that got to do with me?"

The corners of her brother's mouth twitch up into the most boyish, shit-eating grin. He looks more like her brother than he has since she left home. "Not much, truthfully. That's between a man and his wife. But gettin' the marshal called here ain't a good look. 'Sides, you're movin' soon, anyhow."

And she is. She has to. It's a promise she made to herself so long ago she no longer remembers how she phrased the commitment to herself. Is there a loophole Naomi could find if she just remembers exactly how she worded it? *That'd be cheap anyhow. Goin' back on your word.* Even if it was between you and yourself — it's still lowly.

Naomi nods in understanding. She wants too much, too quickly. And Aaron doesn't even know about her true feelings for Clara. The movies that Naomi projects across her ceiling at night of golden hair over a chest, freckled like the Milky Way. Of the sloping plains of her calves or her fingers dancing over bare skin. Worst of all, she wants it all selfishly.

Naomi is leaving soon, and she can't take Clara with her. Nor will she leave herself behind for a married woman.

Winter

Chapter Fourteen

But still, Naomi yearns for Clara. For more nights of falling asleep to Clara's slight snores and watching her rub the sleep from her eyes at the breakfast table. These fantasies conjure a romantic ache in her heart. An ache with no salve, no medicine, except time and distance. Neither of which Naomi is interested in for herself. She wants to imbibe in Clara for as long as she can. It's selfish, and harmful to both of them. But like getting high, to her damaged mind, it soothes the wound without healing it. Over time, Naomi thinks she might forget how bad this situation is.

A tambourine of crunching leaves grows as Clara's bicycle pedals up the drive. Her blue raincoat — since returned to her — is pulled tight over a knit sweater, with earmuffs clamped over her head. The wind ushers in clouds overhead but no rain yet. Clara props her bike against the stairs and opens the front door like a woman come home.

The kettle sings and two mugs of green tea and honey sit waiting for her. The couch is clear of unfolded laundry for what Naomi anticipates to be a long dive into the remainder of the hidden boxes. A hefty pile of splintered logs is stacked on the rocky ledge of the fireplace. Naomi is dressed down in a pair of long johns and a Davis's sweatshirt. Her feet are bare and tucked beneath each leg in a cross-legged sit.

Naomi explains how and where the antique trunks were found, and with it, some background about her family. Her paternal lineage at the church, what little knowledge she has of her Grandma Dottie's witchcraft, and what little else she knows of her mama's side. She's honest with Clara in regard to how much she doesn't know and how much she hopes these boxes will reveal. But Naomi keeps the information short and distant. Her father is briefly mentioned, but she skips over details regarding his temperament and his death, not wanting to get into all of that with Clara.

Naomi starts with the one box she's already opened and shared. She smoked beforehand so ash or ember isn't accidentally flicked onto the precious keepsakes. Her buzz still floats between her ears, but her fingers are steady and careful with each artifact. The photos of Naomi, Aaron, and Grandma Dottie are handed to Clara.

They sit side-by-side, and she points to each face asking who they are. Naomi introduces her friend to each family member but can tell that Clara itches for more. *Do you only have one sibling? Have you always lived here? How often do you see your family?*

Naomi wishes for an open door between them. Especially since, as of late, their relationship is more akin to separate rooms in a large hotel. The information given is vague and softly spoken. *Yeah, just Aaron. All my life. I don't really.*

Clara seems to understand the intent behind the clipped responses and her questioning dies down. The wooden pick between her teeth twitches with each question she holds back.

When they're finished with the first box, they move on to one that Naomi hasn't opened yet. They're greeted by a sepia-toned photograph of Grandma Dottie, Grandpa Richard, Aunt Eda, and Aunt Petunia.

"I don't know much about my kin outside my folks 'n Aaron. Father talked about his side of the family. Particularly, his father and his father's father," Naomi explains. "But we didn't learn much about Mama's family 'sides their names."

Her maternal great-aunts passed years before she was born. Aunt Eda was the oldest, followed closely by Aunt Petunia, then a seven-year gap before Grandma Dottie entered the family. The two eldest sisters moved to Eastfield — a town one county over — when they found themselves engaged and married to a set of friends from there.

In the pictures, the three wear dresses past their knees. Eda and Petunia have their hair pulled into braids, and Dottie has two small pigtails. Their smiles are large and their feet rest in river water. In the next, their mama is there. She splashes water on her children whose hair drip and dresses cling. Written in black ink on the back are their names and the date of the photo: *Eda, Petunia, Dottie, and Opa Curtis, 1955. (Walter)*

Naomi flips each photo to the back of the stack. She didn't even know what her great-grandma's name was before reading it. Naomi hopes that the people in the pictures were as kind as they appear. The next is their father, Walter, and Eda with fishing poles in hand, Dottie beside them with a fish lipped on her thumb. The man in the photo is clean-shaven with only wisps of hair on the top of his head. His eyes are squished at the corners and his mouth hangs open in laughter. His face is slightly blurred as though his joy couldn't be contained within the photo. At the back in cursive: *Eda, Dottie, Walter Curtis. (Opa)*

"It's so amazing she kept these," Clara whispers in awe. "I don't think I have many photos of anyone in my family older than my parents. It's hard to keep track of them, I guess."

"I think Grandma Dottie had to keep 'em hidden. That's why they were in the wall. I don't think—" Naomi pauses, unsure of how to phrase her assumptions about her Grandpa Richard's temper. "I don't think Grandpa Richard liked her family much."

"How could anyone not like them?" Clara picks up the photo of the girls and their daddy with the fish and holds it like a fine piece of silk. "I guess most people are on their best behavior for a photo, but they look so nice."

This was the family that Mama left for Father. That Grandma Dottie left for Grandpa Richard. Naomi's eyes begin to sting. Her great-grandparents passed long ago. The number of years is unknown to her, but it was likely before even her mama's time due to the typical life expectancy in the area. But this man allowed his girls to fish and swim and play wild in the river. This freedom hasn't been enjoyed by her kin in the long years since. *How could they have that and give it up to be with Father or Grandpa Richard?*

To live a life nearly barred from the water or activities outside of the church.

Naomi once asked her mama what the crisscrossed scars on her knuckles were from. Her mama's only response was, "You gotta listen to your father, Naomi." Even as a girl, she knew what that meant. Margaret did not escape the hands of cruel men from childhood to adulthood.

She was simply transferred from one to another. Her mama stayed late at the church sewing group one time and Eddie locked the door and left her out all night. She slept on the porch until morning. After that, she always left early no matter how many of her friends pleaded with her to stay and chat for just a little while longer.

Why? Naomi begs for answers. *Why go to another horrible man?*

Throughout the box, there's only one photo of Grandpa Richard. It was as if he only existed for a moment in Grandma Dottie's life. How could Grandma Dottie give up her family for someone that she wouldn't even keep pictures of? That question isn't answered in this box. The last thing they discover inside it is a bundle of photos only of a young Margaret.

Within Naomi's home growing up, there were no childhood photos of her mama. The pictures in Naomi's hand show a small girl with chestnut hair: short and wavy and a little untamed. There are ones of her at Christmas, dressed for school, and sitting with Grandma Dottie on the blue couch that still resides in the living room.

"You have the same eyes," Clara says softly. It's meant to be a compliment, Naomi knows, but it's a shot in the heart that the likeness must end there.

The final box holds only a few photos, dated between 1903 and 1935. The rest are news clippings and handwritten information. They're loosely bound together with two sheets of leather wrapped in twine. The first piece is ripped from a decades-old edition of a local newspaper, the *Ozark Channel*:

"The Kemiwe *River was the heart of the town, with veins of water curved through the forest between rocky banks and occasional steep bluffs. When the descendants of the current townsfolk arrived in the 1830s, the river was estimated to have been fifty feet wide in some places. In the coming years, they learned that it varied from about twenty-five feet to fifty feet depending on the rainfall of the season and the section of the river. They built their first constructions on the east side of the river on a small ten-foot bluff above a deeper section of the water source. There were a few homes and the first rendition of the Blaire Baptist Church.*

The main waterway received its name — the Kemiwe River — after a ghastly incident involving a woman by the name of Madeline Weir and her husband Kenneth Michael Weir. The two had been married for several years with no luck in growing their family. Kenneth had left his home in eastern Tennessee, within the depth of the Appalachian Mountains, months before he, his wife, and the other migrants arrived in the Ozarks. From one range to another.

The Weir couple traveled in a caravan of thirty-six others from Gretchen, Tennessee, to a green land in the Salem Plateau of south-central Missouri. It was an area plentiful in its lush flora that varied with the same number of green shades as there were stars in their unpolluted sky. From above — although none that lived then or before or for many years to come would know — the Ozarks lifted and dove deep with contours, twists, and turns similar to a brain. A giant connected system of communication could be felt between the many waterways, lush vegetation, plentiful wildlife, vast cave system, and endless spill of milk and glitter sprinkled across the night sky.

It had always been a beautiful and rather eerie place. Well before the Weirs and company arrived, the Ozarks were predominantly home to the Osage and Missouri tribes, who utilized the wealth of game and fishing present in the hills and hollers. The tree trunks back then were thick as the forests were ancient and strong, and they reached to the sky to shade and protect the people below.

Many Native tribes were at home in the hills for thousands of years. However, a steady flow of Europeans made their way through the land. And in the nineteenth century, they began to settle en masse. The French, Scots-Irish, and English — even the Appalachian pioneers who relocated from other areas of the United States — trailblazed their way west.

They tore down the forests that had protected the land and its inhabitants for so long. The cooperative system of intricate give and take, cultivation, and responsibility was decimated for centuries to come. Forests that were old growth, that held trees of such girth that it's difficult to imagine in the Midwest were logged and floated down the timeworn rivers.

The valleys became withered streets of broken pavement, leaving only cracks to take shelter in rather than a lush canopy to shade its inhabitants from the sun. Along with their forest obliteration, the newcomers also brought disease. Different fevers and epidemics overtook the people, with the Native populations suffering the most. As the earliest settlers had set the trend of Revelations-like clouds of pestilence and death, the newer generations of colonizers continued without doubt towards their self-proclaimed manifest destiny and godly Christian wrath. But land does not bow — even to conquerors — and the earthquakes of 1811-1812 quite literally shook the communities to their core.

Not long after the earthquakes in 1811 was the birth of Blaire — 1831 — and the Weir family tragedy. According to local legend, the family of two was praying for a tiny new addition to their family tree. One night, Madeline Weir made supper and invited a charming stranger into their home after she and her husband met him in town. The man — John — was a logger with a penchant for storytelling. Their hospitality was evident the following day when a mob of townsfolk investigated the crime scene.

John murdered them both after their meals. Madeline was hit in the temple with the cast iron cauldron she had used to cook supper. Her face was then bludgeoned with the hot metal until the contents of her skull filled its hollow bowl. Kenneth had his eyes pulled from their sockets and John dragged him as he fought to the river where he tied Kenneth's feet and hands and tossed him in. However, a few fishermen saw the man get tossed into the river. Madeline Weir's whereabouts were investigated soon after. Kenneth Weir's body was never recovered.

While there was ample evidence of the murder, there was little insight as to why. No items had been stolen from the Weir home. John was composed as the mob dragged him to town. It was only known that he declared his innocence with no alibi. Theories ranged from an affair to witchcraft.

After the incident, John was hanged in the town square, and his body was buried outside of the cemetery — unmarked. The town mourned the young couple, and an anonymous stone carver crafted an obelisk of sorts as a gift to the people of Blaire in memory of an important figure in their town's history. The citizens of Blaire welcomed the gift and placed it at the head of the newly designated plot for a graveyard at Blaire Baptist. The obelisk was sandstone with a large cross carved towards its top, and another engraving on the height of its pedestal:

> Who will establish you
> and guard you from the evil one'

Alongside the obelisk, the town also commemorated the man by naming the river he died in after him — however morose the gesture may have been — by using the first two letters of each of his names. The graveyard has fallen into disrepair over the centuries.

Many of the early graves have sunk where the bodies were buried, which has produced an ominous sense that something is missing. John's grave, on the other hand, has never been confirmed. The town never gained enough of a population or fame to ever necessitate a historical dig to find the site. It is assumed by the townsfolk of Blaire that he was somewhere, and that unknown place was fine: out of sight, out of mind."

Naomi passes the sheet to Clara. The Weir story isn't news to her. It is history taught in school. The murder is a scary story told on the playground. However, the use of that specific Bible charm on the obelisk is new information to Naomi. Perhaps it's a coincidence that it's the same charm found in the cross she threw out the day her father died. She continues through the box in search of an answer.

Chapter Fifteen

The second sheet of the aged papers begins with:

"Stories collected and writ by Dorothy Curtis."

There are documents of all different sorts and sizes, lined and unlined. Some dated at the top, some at the end. Each has the signature of whoever's story it was. A few have pictures of the storyteller. They are arranged by date of collection, starting with Great-Grandpa Walter's, the first of which was dated 1965. Clara is entranced by the sepia-toned photos of the bygone eras.

"Walter Charles Curtis. November 17, 1965
Well, I first saw her at school. Her hair was real dark and curly
— like yours. And she was smart as a whip. Opa'd show me how to
curl my letters like the teacher did, real pretty. After school, I'd walk
her home. Some-a-the time she'd hold my hand 'til she thought her

daddy might see. We weren't steady 'til later. I started workin' at the Walker Lumber Company and she helped her mama out at home. Her and her mama and her granny had the gift. Folks'd stop by for Bible charms, medicine, and helpin' with mamas-to-be. Ain't no horseshit neither. They did good by the folks 'round here. Back then Blaire only had them three granny women.

    What 'n the hell you want me to say? We got married in — uh — '38 and I bought me 'n her this house here. Her granny (Dorothy Beckler, b. 1868?) went home to the Lord and so'd her daddy (Seth Beckler, b. 1882) that year, and her mama (Mary Beckler, b. 1893) moved in with us 'til she went in '40. We used to go down to the creek and shoot raccoons and catch catfish. Run on back to the house and cook us up supper. I worked long hours 'for your mama passed, bless her. And bless little Eda for helpin' out like she did. Done right raisin' her. All you girls, we did."

Naomi's first thought was one of relief: *Maybe my hair didn't come from Father after all.*

There were seven stories collected from Great-Grandpa Walter. Two about his past kin, two about Great-Grandma Opa's, two about the Kemiwe and Blaire, and the story of Opa and Walter. These loving but brusque stories told of the Curtis family were none that had been passed to Naomi. *How many stories are lost? How much of my family don't I know about?*

For two hundred years her descendants have inhabited these hollers, and she knows of only a few. Each generation with several members, dating back to the early 1800s, each person with a million stories. All that is left are the ones carefully written on scrap paper and wrapped in dried deerskin by a woman that realized too much of her history had already slipped away.

The loose sheets, when fashioned together like a puzzle, make up the Curtis family tree. Grandma Dottie painstakingly penned, as neatly as possible, each name, birth date, and death date to the best of her knowledge. Some lack middle names, or exact days or months, but the year is always present even if it's followed by a question mark. Under Great-Grandma Opa, it says *October 11, 1965 "bad heart."*

It was no coincidence that Grandma Dottie had begun her compilation of lore and history in 1965. Death can be a great motivator. For Great-Grandpa Walter, it reads *February 02, 1969 "lumber accident."*

Naomi wonders what it's like to lose someone with stories worth collecting. Huge ancestral chunks of her story were snuffed out and only pieces remained. Dottie must have realized all the decades that were lost along with her mama. The particular word choice and vocal inflection her mama would have used to breathe her own essence into those tales and with it the closest-to-truth retelling of her life. While others could try, it would never be the autobiography her own mama would have been able to portray.

Naomi and Clara return the contents to the trunk and turn their attention to the final box. Within are two books: the Bible, and an encyclopedia of native plants. Naomi cradles the latter on her lap and opens it to the first page. It's boxed at the edges and the papers have yellowed with time. Handwriting is inked on each page, little paragraphs and notes. Occasional slips of paper between the pages add additional details and stories about each herb, tree, and flower.

The handwriting differs from page to page. Naomi flips back to the title page and in midnight ink it reads, *"Mary Beckler, Opa, Eda, Petunia, and Dottie Curtis."* In a different ink and handwriting, *"Walter"* is listed after her grandma's name. Not an afterthought, but an inclusion years after the first inscription.

The script of her kin fills each yellowed sheet. Their thoughts on the uses of plants — both native to the Ozarks and species introduced throughout recent centuries. There are discussions in the margins regarding the surest ways to find each herb or how to grow it. On pieces of paper between the pages are instructions on how to create tinctures with certain herbs and what they're best used for.

Naomi knows what a granny woman is. She's heard of them even before seeing the term in the boxes. It's a tradition and practice in the Ozarks carried by women. They have knowledge of healing remedies, herbalism, midwifery, and such. Naomi's father regarded them as practitioners of the left-handed sort: witchcraft.

In a secluded area like Blaire, where it's often difficult to get to a doctor and even more difficult to pay for one, granny women are sought after. However, there hadn't been one in Blaire since long before Naomi was born. Her father spoke of the old granny woman and how all of the "good people" in town had refused to be her student. Her knowledge died with her. Now, with all of Naomi's newfound knowledge about her maternal family, it's undeniable that the last granny woman of Blaire was her Grandma Dottie.

Clara's fingers are gentle with the pages. They trace the words of Naomi's ancestors regarding the pawpaw tree. "We could plant the garden out front based on what you find here. If you want, I'm sure we could keep all the plants local." She hesitates. "If you're interested."

"I'd still like a few things from your seed collection. I doubt they got any hot peppers in this book," Naomi says with a wry smile.

Naomi switches her focus to the Bible while Clara continues to thumb through the encyclopedia. It's bound tightly in brown leather. Its pages are preserved much better than the book prior. It's not marked up like the other either, but contains extra paper clippings with notes. Certain scriptures — or Bible charms — are copied and annotated with their uses.

Naomi remembers this book's contents all too well. Information learned under the penalty of being belted is hard to forget. For so many years, Naomi cast the book aside. It brought her nothing but bruises and loneliness. *Why did the Curtises have to rely on the damn thing, too?*

With her thumb, she flips through the pages quickly. When nothing stands out, Naomi tosses the Bible on the coffee table. When it lands, the book opens itself, as if it's been spread wide on that page so many times before.

Naomi leans over the book to see Thessalonians 2:3-3. Unlike the rest of the Bible, this part of the passage had ink on the page itself. Beside it is a drawing of a figure with fingers like long blades of black wheat that crawl along the edge. The toes are smudged with black ink, and it emerges from a dark, pit-like circle. Red ink underlines:

> *"Who will establish you*
> *and guard you from the evil one'*
> *Thessalonians 2:3-3"*

Above it is one word sketched over and over itself:

HAINT

"Look at this one. I started it but it seems kinda personal." Clara holds a few folded papers out to her. Naomi shuts the book and tucks it back into the trunk in an effort to dissuade her friend from looking. In Clara's hand is another story. This one dated 1968 — a year before Grandma Dottie's daddy's death. It isn't titled at the top, only described as being from the memory of Walter Curtis, scribed by Dottie Curtis.

"Back in the 1830s, Kenneth and Madeleine Weir invited a man named John and his oldest daughter, Anne, to supper. He was from just outside of town. Back then it weren't a state yet. The Osage and the Missouri Indians lived in these hills, too. The forts up north used to trade with 'em. Back 'fore us lumber folks tore it all down. The trees were as tall as the stars and the river weren't named the Kemiwe and it was deep enough for fish to grow half as big as a man. Nobody knows much about [John] or his wife or his children. He left to hunt one day and didn't come back, but Anne did.

She came back to her mama cryin' about somethin' awful happenin' to her daddy. A man attacked 'em at supper. He took his own wife's head in with the hot pot. John defended hisself but Anne couldn't remember it all. She said the man — Kenneth, she said — had eyes green like the grass but they glowed like fire. She couldn't remember all of it. Her daddy woke her up after a while. There was blood everywhere and Kenneth's eyes weren't there no more. John had tied his arms and legs up and [Kenneth] cried for 'em to free him.

Anne'd begged her daddy to let him go but he told her to remember what she saw. The man had attacked first and there was somethin'

On the day her father died, Naomi walked through the
Blaire Baptist Graveyard. The old obelisk stood halved and
brooding, still heads taller than the other gravestones.
Throughout all of the history of Blaire, not one name stood
the test of time greater than the Weirs and their tragedy.
Sure, today it isn't told with remorse or respect for their

founders. It's a ghost story. That even those that shine like gold and speak like wine can turn on you as John had. The mystery of the tale has made townsfolk shiver for two centuries.

And for two centuries a lie has been told to protect two of Blaire's founding members.

Naomi has found several instances of Thessalonians 2:3-3 scattered across town — across the history of Blaire and her kin. Someone illustrated the thing — the *haint* — in her family Bible. But madness can be passed from generation to generation.

Perhaps some of this story stuck to her genetics like the color of her eyes or the curls of her hair and can't be shaken off no matter how much church she does or does not attend. Or perhaps it isn't the story that's attached to her family, but the creature itself.

"Naomi, are you alright?" Clara places her hand on Naomi's knee, but Naomi shakes it off and rushes to pack the boxes. "I'm sorry," she murmurs.

"S'alright. But I'm done with this. I don't even know what we were expectin' to find. Just a bunch of bullshit." Naomi is rough with the papers, shoving them back where they came from, pulling them from Clara's lap. She stands up with the trunks stacked haphazardly in her arms.

As soon as the door is open, Naomi pushes through to lock the history away where nobody will find it again: out of sight, out of mind. Halfway down the stairs, her foot misses a step, and the boxes launch from her grip. She tucks into herself and rolls down the stairs landing on her shoulder with a cry. One of the boxes breaks open and its contents scatter.

"Naomi! Oh God, let me help." Clara runs down the stairs but stops when Naomi continues her angry tirade.

"I don't need it. Fuck!" Naomi pulls herself into a seated position. Her shoulder hollers with strain and so do her knees. She's out of breath and hot tears spill down her cheeks, but the dark basement hides them from Clara. "I'm done with all this family bullshit. I don't wanna learn nothin' 'bout these people. I don't want *you* pryin' where you ought not to."

Clara stands uncomfortably at the top of the steps, a silhouette with sunlight — or maybe firelight — brilliant behind her. She flexes her hands as if searching for the right thing to do with them. "Like I'd stay with you talking to me like that." She turns and leaves.

Naomi hears the rain when Clara opens the front door but does not stop the woman from bicycling home in the icy December downpour.

Chapter Sixteen

There is a long silence in Naomi's house — a silence that stretches for days. She doesn't reach out to Clara after the incident nor venture back to the cellar. The papers and pictures remain littered on the floor like the dead leaves outside. *Winter is an ugly beast*, Naomi thinks. *It's harsh and cold and ugly. There's no life left.* There are no mushrooms or berries to forage in the bitter season. Just frozen ground and the dust of crumpled leaves.

She knows that all the small updates she's completed on the house in the past few months aren't important. None of it was necessary, just fabrications to give her a reason to stay. To stay at Clara's side. Now, she's alone in the old farmhouse, watching television and getting high, waiting for Clara to call and unwilling to make the call herself.

Securely bundled in an old denim coat and perched on her rocker, Naomi holds a joint in her frozen hand and observes Grandma Joyce's familiar beige sedan make its way up the drive. She snuffs out the joint on the bottom of her boot before jogging down the stairs to assist her.

The old woman has a cane now. Yet another reminder of how much of her family's lives are unknown to Naomi. Their greeting is short: relaxed but obligatory. Everyone in the Darby family, except Aaron, has kept their distance from Naomi even since the funeral.

The two sit quietly in the near-empty living room, on opposite sides of the old couch. Joyce babbles about the small comings and goings of her life. Naomi remains silent.

"The place looks real clean." Joyce looks around at the bare walls.

"Thank you."

"Kinda borin' if you ask me." Joyce chuckles. The silence continues.

Long ago, Naomi began to utilize silence as a punishment for unkind or ingenuine comments. Usually, it keeps Naomi from having to be a part of the conversation. She can float away.

"Well, I came here to talk to you 'bout somethin'." Joyce turns to face Naomi. "Your brother is takin' over your daddy's spot at church. Thought you might wanna come support him."

Ah fuck. There really is no escaping old familial paths. "Maybe."

"You know, I think he's been havin' a real hard time. It's a lotta pressure 'n—" she pauses. "Margaret 'n Lily say he's been real restless. Pacin 'n stayin' up all hours of the night. Poor boy! We're all stronger when family's together. Don't you think?"

Silence.

"Naomi, please."

Please, what? Naomi wants to yell. *Please come back. Please be with us. Please sacrifice your progress in leaving and growing to come back to us. The church. Your brother and Mama and Grandma. Be with us. Stay with us.*

"I'm trying to keep us all safe," Joyce pleads.

"Safe from what, Grandma? I'm safe here," Naomi says, her exasperation evident.

Then, Joyce's face changes. Like she wasn't expecting to break through to Naomi. It's been years since a real attempt was even made. Years since birthday or Christmas cards arrived in Naomi's mailbox. A twinkle of fear in Joyce's eyes sparks interest and confusion in Naomi.

"These hills hold things," Grandma Joyce responds. "We both know that. So much life 'n clean water. More animals than we can eat. But in a place with so much life, so much history, other things live too." Joyce holds her cane with white knuckles. "Your father was a bastard of a man. Just like his father," Grandma Joyce whispers.

Never in Naomi's life has *anyone* spoken ill of her father.

"Some think there ain't never been new evil. Just the same old in a new skin. That ain't true. It don't always have to come from somewhere else. I worry that your brother may be battlin' those evils. It's hard to do with a split-up family like ours. I thought I had fought it off a long time ago. But the Lord 'n his ways, you know." Joyce turns the cane's bottom tip in circles on the floor, knuckles tight and gaunt. "Your daddy fought it for a long time. Your leavin' didn't help, you know?"

"Oh, Jesus fuck," and the words are out with no turning back.

"What did you say to me, girl?"

"I want you to leave." The dam has broken, and Naomi no longer sees a reason to try and repress all her anger. With Clara out of her life, she'd be gone soon anyway. She might as well burn it all down before she goes. "And never come back."

"Just like you did to your daddy. I'm gone. Though I had hoped to give you somethin' your—"

"I don't want jackshit from you. I don't even know you. Damn your eyes, get out!" Naomi marches to the front door to prove how serious she is.

Joyce watches her with sharp eyes. She shakily stands. "I just didn't want to be like your daddy or his daddy."

Naomi laughs. "Whatever the fuck that means. Just get out."

Joyce stops in the doorway. "I'll tell you what it means! It means you're just as rotten as your daddy. That evil in him is in you just as deep and you ain't never gettin' rid of it. You… you—" Joyce pauses, flustered. "You're mean. You left us. You left us with him. So now, I'll leave you." She shoves through the door.

"That's all I've ever wanted!" Naomi slams the door. Her heart aches. It was a painful reunion but something in her is… alive. In all her years, in all her dreams, she'd never thought she would be able to say this to any member of her family. All of the loneliness and the guilt and the weight of being a walking sin… lifted. A cool cloth wraps around her heart, and she is calm. It doesn't hurt to hurt.

A blood-curdling scream shreds through Naomi's moment of peace, followed by a rapid series of thuds. Naomi looks through the window to find the old woman's twisted and mangled body struggling for breath at the bottom of the steps. Black wisps of airy tentacle fingers break through her chest and rip her sternum in two.

Out of the inky black pool emerges a creature like the illustration in the family Bible. It pulls itself from her torso like a man buried alive and ravenous for air. Its essence sways as it exits her body and Naomi is too horrified to look away. It continues to float up and up until its feet are obscured by the roof.

When Naomi looks back at Joyce, she is no longer gasping for air. The black hole in her chest is no more.

It takes several minutes before Naomi is able to open the front door. Her stare can't leave the smoke-like toes that float next to the gutter. After a minute, they continue their flight upward and out of sight. Still, Naomi waits. It can't be a coincidence that the first creature she saw made its appearance just days after her father's death and now. She's watched a similar being split Grandma Joyce in half and crawl out of her like a parasite that had taken everything it needed from its host. That evil had lived inside her father, too.

For the first time in years, Naomi takes a moment to pray.

Please, God, let it be gone. Let it be done with me. Let me leave this house in peace. I want to try. I want to try. Don't make me leave her out there like this.

Naomi calls 911 before she pushes the door ajar. It's a quick call. Send someone. My grandma fell. It's an emergency. She isn't breathing. Hang up. Wait.

And they came. Marshal Wilder and the paramedic pronounce her dead on-site. The cause is likely her visibly broken neck. However, that isn't the only damage. Joyce's leg — which had suffered a recent break of the tibia that had only just healed enough for her to start walking again — is splintered. With it snapped the fibula. Both leave a jagged hole through the skin of her right shin. The white bone is a glacier in the dark sea of blood and torn flesh.

Several fingers are bent at unnatural angles. The broken glass of her bifocals is partially lodged into her eyes, which were once brown but now glassy and gray in death. The skin of her neck stretches like taffy across shattered bone and ruptured ligaments. There are ripples across her throat like gills, brought on by her head being turned nearly one hundred and eighty degrees. She lies on her stomach, but her eyes look to the sky. To that *thing*.

Despite all of Joyce's injuries, she survived for a minute, maybe two, after the fall. Enough for her adrenaline-rushed heart to pump hot blood out of each wound to steam off the cold gravel. The paramedic says that blood lingers in the rocks like that. That it might be best to get rid of that section and replace it.

The marshal asks many questions. What she and her grandma were speaking about. If the visit was unusual. If Naomi was beside her when she fell. Naomi couldn't help but think that the investigation was narrowing its eyes at her. And she remembers the gentle hand that wrapped up her heart in the comfort of telling Joyce to *finally fuck off*. She hopes the marshal can't hear her thoughts. Or the speed that her heart is thumping:

Guilty.
Guilty.
Guilty.

The weight of sin and cruel hope sits on her shoulders like a bully trying to make her eat mud on the playground. Naomi spent years distant from her family. Hating them but never telling them. *For good reason*, she reminds herself. *I hate them for good reason. I stayed for good reason.* But the guilt and the fear build up and all she wants in the whole world is for Clara to cup her beautiful hands and let Naomi pour it all out for her friend to hold and share.

"Alright, I think we're done for now." Marshal Wilder tucks his notepad into his shirt pocket and turns to the scene of the crime.

"What else will you need?" Naomi sits on her rocking chair, curled into herself.

"Gotta tell your mom and brother. File the report and wait for the autopsy." His boots make a heavy *thump* with every step he takes.

"Alright."

"Before I leave, there anything else you wanna tell me?" He turns and squints at her. Naomi knows that it isn't because of the sun.

She shakes her head.

"If you think of anything, call." And then they are gone. Everyone is gone except the deep red crater at the bottom of her stairs.

It's time for a smoke.

And to finally see Clara.

Chapter Seventeen

Naomi doesn't leave the house for the rest of the day. She doesn't rehearse how she'll tell Clara the news. With the curtains pulled and a fire roaring, she doesn't know why it hasn't entered her home, but she can't bring herself to risk leaving yet. This is the evil her Grandma Dottie, her aunts, great-grandparents, John, and Anne tried to protect folks from. Is Clara's home somehow safe like hers?

All night she waits and ruminates on what lurks outside. The tips of her nails dig into the skin above her hangnails. She tears at them one by one. The unknown is poison. *Why the fuck is it waiting?* She tells herself that when the sun comes up, she will go find out. No more sitting.

But the sun rises on empty trees and frosted grass. It tracks higher and higher in the sky. It melts the ice crystals from the yard. Still, Naomi doesn't leave. All day and all night and all of the next day, Naomi curls into herself inside her house and listens to the tapping of the creature's feet on her roof. It hovers above her. It waits for *something*.

After four months of seeing the creature — creatures? — Naomi still knows so little about them. Even with Grandma Dottie's notes and the details in the margins of a book, she is still hunted, preyed upon.

Despite having no guidance or clues as to how to handle or escape her father, Naomi did it. The first day she could, she left and never looked back. Fleeing was the best option. But now, hiding from the sun in her living room, and the two people she cares most for ignorant of the evil that's living in their woods, Naomi knows that running isn't an option this time. Not if she wants to save them.

That thing — *a haint*, she reminds herself — ripped itself from Grandma Joyce's chest. Surely, the one she saw before on the river bottom, on the bank, and past her driveway were all haints. Maybe those three instances were even the exact same entity. They looked the same. Taller than any person she's ever seen. Maybe seven or seven and a half feet tall. Its fingers like scythes, long and pointed.

Naomi grips her keys between her fingers like claws and runs like a bat out of hell to her truck. With trembling fingers, she locks herself inside and starts the engine. Above her bedroom, on the second floor, is the haint. It's taken on the appearance of a naked, sexless, withered crone. Its signature green eyes are closed. As if it isn't interested in her. Naomi wonders again: *what the fuck is it waiting for?*

Whether there is one or hundreds, it got inside Grandma Joyce somehow. It had a reason for being inside of her. And now, it's out and possibly looking for another host.

A host is her best guess, anyhow. She thought it reminded her of a parasite before. If it is in fact looking for another host to inhabit, she thinks that might imply that it *needs* a person. That could explain why it insists on tapping on her windows and hovering outside her house.

But if Naomi has been chosen to be the haint's next host, what is stopping it?

Naomi races to Clara's house. She parks the truck on the driveway just out of view of the cabin. Fear grips her. If she knocks on the door, then Clara will see her in all of her reclusive self-loathing: dark bags under her eyes, her hair slicked with grease, and her breath reeking.

In Clara and Ethan's bedroom window, Naomi sees Ethan. Even from this far, she can tell his face is beet red and filled with fury. He appears to be yelling but Clara is nowhere to be seen. He's gone for a minute. He returns with Clara in tow, dragging her by the forearm. She resists and he yanks her to him, screaming in her face.

Naomi is out of the truck and slipping between trees before he shuts his mouth.

His raised voice reverberates against the window, too muffled to be made out exactly. Clara pulls her arm from his grip and runs out of the room. Ethan begins to cry as he sits on the edge of the bed. Naomi crouches down about fifty feet from the home, tucked behind a toolshed. Clara appears in the kitchen window. Her hand shakes as she fills a glass with water. The haint might not be the only thing Clara needs rescuing from tonight.

The sound of something sharp tapping on glass draws Naomi's gaze upward. At Ethan's window is the creature. The haint's scraggly, gray hair covers its descended breasts and floats as if it's suspended in water. The verdant glow of its eyes reflecting off the glass illuminates its long silhouette.

Ethan's head jerks up at the tapping. He's still for only a moment before standing up from the bed. Naomi expects him to run from the room or freeze in fright or scream. But instead he shuffles to the window where the haint is waiting. He fiddles with the latches and opens the panel, then backs out of sight. The haint slithers down the window and floats inside. The overhead light flickers off above the bed, plunging the pair into darkness.

Without considering the risks, Naomi sprints to the front door. *It fucking followed me*, she cries to herself. *I fucking brought it to her. It's all my fault.*

Carefully, Naomi turns the knob and nudges the door open. Each footstep within the home is a potential landmine. The house is still. She moves with her back to the wall, taking short side steps towards the kitchen. Her eyes never leave the stairs, waiting for the haint to glide down the ceiling toward her. Quickly, she turns her gaze toward the kitchen to find it empty.

Fuck.

Around the corner, Naomi finds the dining room empty as well. The upstairs remains silent. Naomi begins a creeping ascent up the steps. Each one brings her closer to something she has avoided and denied for many months.

Why'd Ethan willingly approach it? Was that why John 'n Great-Grandpa Walter said to damage its eyes? Could the haint do somethin' with them? Get a person to do somethin'?

Months ago on the Kemiwe, when Naomi fell in and saw the two glowing green lights, she froze. She nearly let herself drown because of how they hypnotized her. That was until her vision was disrupted. Once she couldn't see the green lights, the spell was broken. She curses herself for being stupid enough to think it was all meaningless folktales.

In Great-Grandpa Walter's telling of the story, John wrangled Kenneth Weir and drowned him in the river. *How do I get the haint bound and down to the river?*

Naomi is halfway up the stairs now and she peers through the bars of the wooden railing into one of the bedrooms. All of the lights are off, and still no sign of either of the home's occupants.

"Naomi?"

She drops into a squat and whips around to face Clara at the foot of the stairs. Her friend's eyes are wide with concern. The signature toothpick is missing from her mouth. *Is she really that comfortable right now? Doesn't even need her fix?*

Naomi races down as quietly as she can and reaches out to hold Clara, but the woman takes several steps back. She bumps into the backside of the couch.

"Naomi, why are you here?" Clara's voice shakes.

"Clara, I—" She doesn't know what to say. What is there to say? She could pour her heart out about how right Clara was about *something* being in the woods outside Naomi's house that night they spent together. That it's *inside* Clara's home as they speak. She could cry and fill the space between them with tearful apologies and tell the truth about covering it all up. About not believing it herself. She could have brought the letter. That would have been some kind of proof.

But instead, Naomi inhales deeply and her hands quake and the hair on her neck stands on end. And she says nothing.

"Naomi, you need to leave," Clara says.

"Clara, no. Please. Somethin's here. In the house. I saw it in the window." Naomi's voice is hushed and sharp.

"You need to go." Clara backs away around the couch. Naomi follows.

"Somethin' happened 'n I owe you the truth—"

"I know your grandma died. I know you were there, Naomi."

Oh. She recognizes the fear in Clara's eyes. The clench of her jaw and the way her fingernails dig into her palms. Naomi stops approaching and steps backward, so the couch separates them.

"She fell down the stairs, Clara. I'm not here about that. The night we heard somethin' outside — the night I said somethin' was outside — I was full of shit when I said it was nothin' 'n I'm so sorry."

"I know there was nothing out there. I got scared. I know it wasn't anything."

"No, Clara. There *was* somethin'. I've seen it before. I saw it tonight. You were right. I lied. I'm sorry. I shouldn't've done that. I was wrong but, please, we gotta go. It's not safe—"

"Clara? Everything alright?" Ethan's voice booms through the still house and both women nearly jump out of their skins.

Naomi looks back at Clara with pleading eyes. Clara looks back, her expression unreadable. "Yeah, it's alright," she responds to Ethan. She stiffens and directs her words at Naomi next. "You gotta go. You shouldn't be here."

"No!" Naomi hisses. "Please, Clara. I know I fucked up, but it isn't safe here. This ain't right. He ain't right." *For you.*

"He's just fine." *For me*, Naomi infers. "Leave." Clara's voice is hard as granite and final. A creak on the steps shatters what hope Naomi has left. She bolts out the front door and through the lawn. She runs all the way to her truck. From the safety of her locked cab, she weeps for Clara, for God, then she drives home.

A cold settles under Naomi's skin. The initial icy panic of her Grandma Joyce's fall hasn't faded with the rise and fall of another day. It's a bullet that doesn't come out the other side. It keeps and it festers, and she shivers from infection under her blankets. However strong this one emotion is, it's the only thing present. There is no sensation of the soft cotton against her bare skin. Her tongue hasn't moved since the last words she spoke to Clara. Whether it's dry or not isn't a sensation that Naomi can process.

Are her eyes bloodshot? Is she holding her own arms too tightly and bringing on bruises? Answers to these are neither sought nor considered. And they will be lost by morning.

Naomi floats. Her thoughts are smoke in the wind — gone before their shapes can form. That cold is all that is left of her perception of the evening. Guilt is stowed away for the time being. For when Clara is with her again. Clara will help. She always does. Naomi has hours — days? — to wait.

But time doesn't exist in the same capacity for Naomi right now. It twists and curls into an inescapable bramble. She is bound tightly where she lays, moonlight pouring through the window to cover her. She stares blankly, without truly seeing, at her ceiling. At the stripes of light from the moon that migrates so slowly across the room. She registers the passage of time in flashes, sharp movements —

abrupt changes of a foot or so at a time — coming back to the present after bouts of dissociation.

These short snaps in and out of reality give her a vague understanding of the present, past, and future. She simply breathes and blinks.

The awkward angle where the wall meets the ceiling makes the rectangular shape of the window appear bent and larger than it is. Stillness and silence swallow Naomi for hours. Then a bump appears at the bottom of the window's shadow on the wall. It's small at first. Barely blocking any light.

Still, Naomi's mind remains blank. More moonlight is blocked. And more, and more. The haint now blocks the window completely and its shadow is cast on the wall across from her bed. It looks like it did when it ripped itself from Grandma Joyce's soul: a colorless void. The shadow continues to grow and slide up the wall and across the ceiling. It bends grotesquely where the wall and ceiling meet, a sharp break in the spine of the creature that hovers outside Naomi's window. Those disgusting feet dangle, long fingers lay to its side. This is the closest Naomi has ever been to *it*.

Her day had been marred by its ugly form, burnt into her memory in all of its gory detail. Its slippery form hovering and slinking over the roof and into Clara's bedroom. Naomi knows that at that moment, her body was full of rage and horror. Now, she's cut herself off from all of that fear. Naomi isn't capable of an appropriate reaction. She has no sense of preservation — neither fight *nor* flight. There is only floating. So, she waits.

This state of stagnation is where she has always been and where she has never wanted to be. A soft nudge of sorrow at her heart tells her that she has missed all of her chances to flee. Kansas City is the myth now.

Tonight, she resigns to let that *thing* have her if that's what it wants, whatever fate it has planned for her. Whatever deep layer of Hell it has reserved for her.

Her grave will be in that cemetery right beside her father and his father and his father before him.

And whatever is *knock, knock, knock*ing at the window will be the cold, sharp hand to escort her down the same path.

Chapter Eighteen

By morning the haint is gone and Naomi finally erects the for-sale sign. The realtor's enthusiasm and Naomi's exhaustion make for a grueling day.

"Property near water always sells," Rita Platte exclaims. "Especially since it's cheaper for folks to buy a vacation property by one of the rivers than Lake of the Ozarks!"

It's all the same salesman bullshit to Naomi. It's the start of the new year and Rita reeks of first-quarter sales goals. Red coffin-shaped nails grip the hammer as it whacks away at the white sign at the end of Naomi's driveway. The timing is poor, must look suspicious to the marshal, but there's evidence of her desire to run that goes back years, and she can't stay any longer.

The house is presentable enough — family photos still scattered over the basement floor aside. Rita prattles about each room and "the charm, oh, the charm!" as she takes pictures of each original door, floor, and amenity. She explains the process again — to Naomi's dismay — before leaving. An inspector is scheduled to arrive within the week so the process can really move forward.

A week turns into three. "Besides," Rita had told her, "You oughta get the hole in the basement patched before he gets here."

Waiting is exactly what Naomi had hoped to avoid. Time spent alone with her thoughts and fears and self-loathing. Every extra day in Blaire is a nail in the bottom of her foot. It's been over five months since the August day when Eddie Darby was put in the dirt. Surely bugs have found a way in through weaknesses in his pine prison and feast on his bloated, rotting corpse. Naomi doesn't know how the decomposition process actually goes. How long does it take for a coffin to break down? Does it take years for the bones to become exposed? Do eyes last very long underground? Is it hot in that box or is it cold? Naomi hopes it's hot.

Her days are spent looking for rental properties. The savings Naomi built over years of work has dissipated to what will cover maybe three more months and move-in costs. She tries to find suitable areas in the state she can afford that also have the right look.

She hasn't been to many places in her life. A road trip years ago with Erica to Austin, Texas; a few excursions to Arkansas, Kansas City, and Branson. Nowhere else has ever felt quite right, although Naomi doesn't know what right would feel like. Wool socks warmed by a fire? That first hit after a long day?

Rural areas by the city call to her but in all her searching of Missouri, she can't find another town with the nature she longs for.

"The Ozarks lifted and dove deep with contours, twists, and turns similar to a brain. A giant connected system of communication could be felt between the many waterways, lush vegetation, plentiful wildlife, vast cave system, and endless spill of milk and glitter sprinkled across the night sky." The clipping from the *Ozark Channel* that Grandma Dottie saved said it better than Naomi thinks she ever could herself.

Unlike cities that replace all the green with brick and concrete. Or areas with only wide-open lakes or fields like a mouth to swallow you up. Life in the plains seems too exposed. It serves a purpose and can be beautiful in its own right — but the trees are home. The woods give its residents shade, rain protection, and places to hide. In the forest, she is an animal alongside the black bears, opossums, and woodpeckers. Blaire is the only place in the whole state where she can add elk and wild horses to that list.

So, she looks at apartments, townhomes, and houses hoping to find something that sets off an alarm, some sensation that lets her know that she's found what she's been looking for. Living near people doesn't seem so scary when they're new — when they are strangers. Neighbors could become acquaintances, could become friends. And that is an inviting thought.

She thought that perhaps her community in Blaire was looking up, only to sink again. Clara isn't with her anymore. Aaron hasn't visited Naomi since Grandma Joyce died. Hasn't even called.

Does he think Naomi is at fault too? *But he's my little brother.*

But that sentiment didn't mean much when they were little. Why would it mean anything now?

One of the tasks that Rita listed for Naomi is to gut the garden, insisting that cleaning it up will make a difference to buyers. In Naomi's mind, though, doing so isn't supposed to be a chore, but a promise to be fulfilled from early in her relationship with Clara.

Naomi taught her friend the basics of how to swim, but her thumb was still a dead shade of gray when it comes to gardening. And this won't be what Clara had promised her: a revitalization of her Grandma Dottie's pride and joy. It will be destruction, as far as Naomi is concerned.

In denim overalls, gloves, and work boots, Naomi kneels on frigid ground and yanks the dead sprawls of herbs and fruit bushes out of the earth. They are tossed into a haphazard hill over the fence. A pile of bones from a once loved and meticulously groomed family plot. Her forearms ache from the strain.

When it's finished, Naomi sits in an empty graveyard. The dirt itches at her collar and her nose. She wonders how many of the plants floated in as seeds over the years and came to rest in the garden. How many were hand-placed by her Grandma Dottie?

For years, Naomi had known a day would come when Blaire would be in the rearview mirror. When this house would not be hers, this garden would belong to someone else. Despite thousands of days of knowing this, the end of the preparation to hand it off to the next person makes her yearn for family.

Naomi strikes the loose earth with her trowel in frustration. A sharp crash of glass breaks the winter silence. She uses the tool to scoop aside small clumps of dirt until shards of green glass come with it. An old soda bottle, its neck shattered from the force of the trowel. With gloved hands, she pulls the shrapnel out of the garden and, in the thickest part of the bottle, she spies a rolled piece of paper. Like a message in a bottle that might wash up on a beach.

Inside is Grandma Dottie's tight and rolling handwriting.

'Dorothy Curtis-Cleary, 1973

I tried keeping a diary back when Maggie was first born. Richard found it. He gave me a licking for keeping secrets. Since, I've been keeping all my stories in my head. But they've been washing away the longer I wait. The older I get. My baby won't get to learn what my mama and daddy taught me. I grew up God loving, not God fearing. I'm ashamed I haven't given that to her.

I love her. I do. And I kept her as I was told was best. As soon as I was eighteen, I took Daddy's truck to Springfield to see a doctor about making sure I wouldn't get pregnant. That pill was a new thing back then around 1967. I went on my first date with Richard in 1969. He seemed like a real nice boy. He picked me flowers and we went swimming. A month later, I didn't bleed. A month after that, I didn't again. I drove to Springfield and saw that doctor and he confirmed it.

Once my belly started to get round, everybody in town had an idea about what I ought to do. The reverend most of all. It was like all I ever knew about God was gone. It was all taken over by this cruel creature the reverend swore up and down about. He got Richard in on it, too. They'd keep me at the church for hours, scaring me until I couldn't hardly keep my eyes open.

The only time I ever saw my daddy cry was when I told him I was gonna marry Richard. He told me I didn't have to. That he'd do whatever it took. That God wasn't like what the reverend or Richard told me. That he was like Daddy and Mama and Eda and Petunia.

Most folks in town don't want much to do with me no more. There was one gal — Joyce Darby, the reverend's wife — she told me in secret that she was pregnant before she was married, too. Leave it to a man to condemn and sin in the same breath. Joyce says the reverend gets mad like Richard does and that's why she misses Wednesday service sometimes but that he makes her get fixed up for Sunday.

I ain't ever told, but Joyce said sometimes he gets so mad his eyes turn green like they're on fire and I told her that Richard's do, too. I remembered what Daddy told me about John and Anne and I wondered how them eyes got from there to here and how many of them haints there's been. I wonder if I could ever get away with killing Richard. John couldn't, so I don't see why I'd be different. Besides, ain't it better for Maggie to grow up with him as a daddy than no daddy at all?

I miss my friend. Joyce made my days easier when I was pregnant, but it didn't take long before the reverend must have asked his wife to leave me be, since she started ignoring me at service. She was awful nice for a while, but I've learned better than to think those things last.

I keep in this garden as much as I can. Richard doesn't seem to like it over here. Daddy always said the pawpaw protects and attracts spirits. That's why there's always swallowtail butterflies by them — those are the spirits. Maybe Daddy and Mama are shooing Richard away from the garden — from me. I hope they watch for Maggie, too.

I love my daughter. But I wish I had stayed back home and raised her. I don't think I can change that now. How do I keep the evil in this world from getting her when I can't even keep her father from hurting us? I fear they're one in the same. I fear I have damned my whole lineage by letting this evil in.

God willing, we will know peace somewhere."

Naomi stands from the garden and walks her muddy boots all the way to the cellar and the broken boxes that hold her family's secrets. She carefully gathers the photographs and the letters. Each is stacked on top of the encyclopedia of local plants and the Curtis family Bible. At the top, she places Grandma Dottie's newest entry. Naomi carries them back up the stairs and sets them on the kitchen counter.

On the grocery list pinned to the fridge with a sunshine magnet, Naomi writes "fireproof box."

Naomi's farewell from Clara was a cold one. Not a farewell at all, really. Each night since, it's replayed in a torturous loop. Despite how many hours she's spent ruminating, she can't find a way around the actual turn of events. Clara *was* in danger. What could Naomi have done to convince her friend of that? She understands Clara's fear. But at what point is it acceptable for Naomi to say to hell with her friend's perception of events, and save her?

That gives Naomi pause. Like an electric stove on high heat, a sizzling metal coil spins up and up in her stomach to her chest to her throat. An inferno of rage and despair and embarrassment. Is this what her father felt? This need to protect her and her brother, her mama, and all of his congregants from damnation? Was it a sense of vigilante religious fervor that drove Eddie to do the merciless things he did in the name of God? Or was it in the name of power alone?

Naomi cornered the woman she loves in her living room just a day after Grandma Joyce was found dead on her own property. Of course Clara was unwilling to go with her. Even if Naomi had evidence of Ethan not being alone upstairs — of possession — it would be a shot in the dark. All the right in the world can't undo that fear.

No, Naomi decides. *I wasn't like him. Because I left.* It was like abandoning a limb to a bear trap, but she did it. And despite the agony, she knows it was right. That night, Naomi was scary. She terrorized Clara. And maybe Naomi was right to try, but she was also right to leave.

Naomi can see all the wrong in Clara's relationship with Ethan and she can express this to Clara, but what else was there for her to do? What could Dottie have done to keep her mama from Eddie? What could Dottie's daddy have done to keep her from Richard? Naomi supposes it is Clara's right to be with Ethan, and the best thing she could have done is act as a source of kindness and love and safety when Clara needed it.

Grandma Dottie stayed with Richard because she felt it was right — necessary. With their shared blood and baggage, Naomi can look back on that decision with disgust and fury. But what could those around Dottie have done? Should Walter have kidnapped her? Locked his daughter away in her childhood room?

And what could Dottie have done? In a time and a town that withheld her rights from her. That enforced laws that kept her with her bastard of a husband. Even in the worst situations, there is comfort in stagnation. Like the water that is kept far from the flow of the current. It gathers heavy moss and leeches and bacteria, growing warm from the sun and undisrupted by that rush of icy water upstream that forces the river to keep going no matter what. That shocks you into change.

That's where Naomi is — stuck in that nasty, mossy little pool. Stuck with the bloodsuckers and flesh-eating bacteria. With churchgoers that gossip and a father that locked her and her brother away when they disobeyed. Even after she escaped — here she is. A few miles down the road just sitting on her thumbs and waiting. Even after Eddie died. It never changed. Why did she expect a stagnant pool to become a lake? An ecosystem that supports itself. That cleanses its waters of the disease, and houses fish and beavers and turtles.

Naomi knows it's more nuanced than that. Her stillness isn't just fear. Her heart aches for the Kemiwe and the pine trees and the Ozark Mountains even when she's only a step away.

It's a similar ache to what she felt with her too-small Mary Jane's as her father held her wrist tight and dragged her to the cellar. He was the boogeyman, but he was Father, too. Naomi wanted to call him Daddy like the other kids called their fathers. She wanted to go on fishing trips and get band-aids when she scraped her knees.

Fear took a long time to swallow everything else she felt about her father. How can she fault Clara for taking time, too? Or Grandma Dottie or Grandma Joyce or her mama? Well, she will continue to lay blame when it comes to Grandma Dottie and Grandma Joyce and Mama. Naomi knows that the boiling pot of anger that she never allows to cool will keep her from repeating their missteps.

Clara will never find comfort resting her head on a pillow beside all of Naomi's rage while her own fear and resentment eat everything she holds in her heart for Ethan. Naomi's silence, seething contempt for her family and their history, will not benefit anyone. Not her own kin nor Clara. What they both need is a break from the pain and the hurt. Security.

Maybe, Naomi considers, *I'll get her a little pawpaw tree.*

Chapter Nineteen

The oranges and yellows of the fire lick the top of Naomi's stone fireplace. It grows taller as the blanket of snow outside thickens. Her concern for Aaron and his little sedan increases in tandem. It isn't a long trek from his place — or the church if that's where he's headed from. However, there's no team to treat the country roads. Residents either own a truck, suck it up with their little cars, or stay at home. Folks walk if they really need to.

She supposes he will, too, if he wants. The possibility makes her stomach clench. *This isn't that important.*

With sweaty hands, Naomi called her brother an hour after digging up the glass bottle from the garden. She can't fight the current that's carrying her, or she will fall still in the pool again. Aaron agreed to see her that evening, but as the snow starts to cover the top of the dead grass of the yard, so does her guilt. Soon, she'll look her brother in the eye and tell him about Grandma Dottie's family history and the cycle of abuse on both sides of their kin. She will demand that he do something in the congregation to change things.

Yet, Naomi feels like she's about to pop her father in the face. Like Aaron will grow taller and wider and his hair will vanish and his face crack with wrinkles. He will yell and preach and "damn her eyes" for trying to coerce him into destroying their family legacy. He will drag her several miles to that old, familiar root cellar. Her fingernails will dig at the dirt and rocks to stop. They will rip off and leave bloody trails to that damned hole in the ground.

He will lock her away for good. Clara won't know where she is and likely no longer cares. And neither will anyone else. Naomi will weaken and wither until she is nothing but bones and brittle hair. Like her father's corpse, her eyes will rot until there is nothing but empty sockets with maggot eggs. Naomi's part in their family story is just a sad paragraph in an otherwise repetitive tale of a God-fearing family.

But it's high time someone confronted how hypocritical and cruel the tale really is. Naomi knows Aaron won't immediately take to the idea of outing their father as a hateful, beast of a man. She also knows there will be a backlash to any picture painted of the reverend that isn't framed in gold. Marshal Wilder likely attends service each Sunday and the occasional Wednesday. Will Clara be there too?

An upbeat knock wakes Naomi from her spiraling anxiety. Through the window, she sees a trail of footsteps in the snow leading to her porch. Her fingers begin to pick at her hangnails.

"I brought some cobbler this time. I figured you might need it." Aaron's eyes are wide with concern and his smile is tight like an anchor line. He hangs his coat on the rack and continues inside.

"I gotta talk to you about somethin'." It's better to get on with it. That way if it goes south, at least it'll happen fast.

"Sister, it's alright. I spoke to the marshal. While he is mighty concerned about you interferin' with his 'n Clara's marriage 'n your usin' drugs, he don't think you're a murderer. 'Sides, Grandma Joyce just found out she had a calcium deficiency, the doctor said." He sets the berry cobbler on the counter and withdraws a knife from a drawer. He carves a slice for each of them. As if he isn't talking about the possibility of his sister — the person he's sharing a room with — being a suspect in their grandma's death.

"It's awful that these old folks refuse modern medicine. They cling to the old ways like flies to a spiderweb. I told her she needed more rest. She broke her leg just a few months before. Stubborn as all get out."

Naomi's eyes fill with tears, overwhelmed by his understanding and faith in her. She fears most of all that they are from her own guilt. "I'm sorry."

A warm hand holds her own. "I know you are. She's somewhere better, so don't fall in too deep." Aaron tries his best to provide a comforting smile. "Now, I shouldn't've told you all that, so don't go tellin' nobody else."

She sniffs snot back into her nose. "Nobody to tell."

"What about Clara? Isn't she your friend?"

Naomi shakes her head and picks at the cobbler. It might as well be gopher guts. "I wasn't very nice to her when she was here last."

"I imagine you don't feel much inclined to be nice to any of us. We haven't really been family in a long time." His voice is remorseful. Naomi marvels at how far the apple has fallen from the tree.

"No, we haven't. But I never thought that fell on you. Ever. I need you to know that, Aaron. You're my brother. My *little* brother. I hardly know you now. You're married 'n old—" He laughs at that. A loud cackle where he holds his chest as if to keep it in. "And I left you with *him*." The laughter stops abruptly. There is no turning back. "I'm sorry."

"It didn't change after you left, you know." Naomi looks up at her brother and his eyes are downcast. The cobbler is gone, and he wrings his hands. "You leavin' didn't change nothin'. Didn't make it better or worse. I just — I just felt you oughta know."

A rift that Naomi has felt between them for the entirety of their lives as siblings shifts. Part of her always knew that their father's separate treatment and punishment of them had nothing to do with her. He was preparing them for vastly different lives. Aaron was meant to transform from coal into a diamond. His pain converted to sermon.

But Naomi's suffering was to silence her. To create a dutiful wife and mother. It wasn't chess where her moves influenced her father's. He was master and creator of the game. "I'm still sorry. I'm sorry I never told. I could have."

The rogue smile returns to Aaron's face, and he shrugs. "Would anyone've done anythin'?"

It's the truth. She knows he's right. But things have changed. Their father is no longer the reverend. "You could do somethin'." Grandma Dottie's letter rests on the mantle of the fireplace. She retrieves it and hands it to Aaron to read.

The decades-old paper crinkles in his large hands. It fills Naomi with pride that he can look so much like their father and yet be nothing like him. Aaron sits with the letter for a while. Long enough that she figures he must be reading it at least twice.

"Thank you," he says solemnly.

"Aaron," Naomi starts. Her hands are slick with sweat. "You gotta do somethin'. They all look to you now. There are so many folks — *our* folks — that've been hurt by people leadin' the church in bad faith. I still don't like any of it, I'll be honest. But you're as much her 'n Great-Grandpa Walter as you are Father 'n Grandpa Richard. This is all on you now."

Naomi had imagined the speech she would give to her little brother. As if she were on a stage with a microphone in hand. Or she was a doctor on one of her favorite shows and it was up to her to convince someone to do the risky life-altering procedure. She knows it's too dramatic. That her imagination paints pictures of heroes and villains and it's all black and white and *so easy*. But it isn't. Her armpits are damp and her heart races. Aaron could laugh at her. He could tell her in his Christian way, to fuck off. But she can't be silent anymore.

"You're right, sister." Aaron takes a deep breath and his chest puffs. He slaps his hands down on his thighs and meets Naomi's hopeful gaze. "It's on me now."

Chapter Twenty

As Naomi's days in Blaire — and more importantly to her, near the Kemiwe — draw closer to the end, she finds herself drawn to the icy rolling waters. The cold months are usually when she steers clear. Falling in at this time of the year is dangerous. To the untrained, only seconds in the frigid river can turn your muscles to stone and sink you to the bottom. A person must quickly swim and kick to the side, abandoning their raft, and watch whatever goods they had float downriver. Typically, Naomi scoffs at the idea of having a life jacket, but in these months, she smothers her pride and at least stuffs it under the canoe seat.

Ryan helps her bring the *Davis* to the water. The two share a joint and he laments the days when he had a buddy to work with. So does she.

The tackle box rests on the floor at Naomi's feet while the rod lies beside her. The water ripples around her rubber-coated calves as she walks the craft in. She follows the riffles up the slow-moving current of the Kemiwe. With the trees bare, she is left exposed. *I could see another haint,* Naomi considers, but she can't stomach not enjoying every second she has left with her beloved river. The creature seems less daunting now that she knows that it possesses via eye contact.

Up the river maybe half a mile, Naomi spots another of *Davis's* canoes resting on the shore without a rower in sight. Then, Naomi hears crying. She beaches herself beside the other canoe and follows the sound. Behind the tree line squats Clara, leaning against the trunk of a thin tree.

"Clara?"

"Oh Jesus Christ," comes the muffled but irate response.

"It's fine. I'll leave you to it." Naomi begins to leave when Clara turns to her.

"I need you to hold my hair," Clara mumbles. "Please."

In front of the woman is a pile of vomit. Bits of food and stomach acid cling to her bronze strands and tears stain her cheeks. "I don't wanna get anymore in my fucking hair, you know?"

Naomi steps forward. With both hands, she scoops Clara's long hair off of her neck. She sweeps her face for leftover strands and gently holds it all in a knot at the back of her head. Each time Clara's head tips forward toward the rocks, Naomi tries to follow her just enough that she doesn't pull her hair. Her locks are soft, and she feels like a creep noting the detail during such a vulnerable moment.

After several rounds of vomiting, Clara sprawls over the rocks. "I think I'm good for a bit."

"Lemme get some of that outta your hair," Naomi offers, and leads Clara to the river's edge. Her hair is long enough to reach the water without her body getting wet. Naomi cups her hands full of the icy liquid to clean the strands by her face. Bronze ropes are wet to black and small chunks of scum sail away down the river. Naomi uses her fingers to break apart anything that resists. Then she uses the back of her canvas coat to dry Clara's hair slightly. "You need somethin' for your stomach?"

"Medicine can't fix it," Clara retorts. "I'm pregnant." She backs herself to the side of the canoe and squats down. Like an opossum baring its teeth from a corner.

Naomi shuffles her feet and keeps quiet. She repeats yesterday's lesson to herself: *the best thing I can do is be a source of kindness and love and safety when Clara needs it.*

"Congratulations."

"Why'd you lie to me?" Clara counters.

"'Bout what?" Naomi's skin turns yellow and her voice weakens.

"The night at your place, you said you didn't see anything, didn't know anything. Either you lied then, or you lied that night when you got into my house. Which was it?" Clara's voice is pepper spray, brass knuckles. A self-defense mechanism that Naomi's never seen her display. Naomi knows that she deserves it. She hopes that others that deserve it get their licks, too.

Clara reaches into her pocket with a shaky hand. She withdraws her little plastic tube of toothpicks and pops one between her teeth. Naomi tries not to dwell on what it means. What Clara might be trying to distract herself from. Or yearning for.

"At my place. I'd seen it before. In the woods, outside my window, here at the river," Naomi confesses. "I don't think I've really seen it since the night I went to your house though."

Clara looks up at her, eyes devoid of their usual soft and forgiving light. "That is a really weird way to put that, and I'll get back to that in a minute. But you made me think I was crazy. You got mad at me for trying to learn about it. You left me alone with it — with the idea of it in my fucking head."

"I know," Naomi coughs up.

"You know a lot of fucking things, don't you?" Clara rubs her forehead roughly and sighs.

"I shouldn't've lied. I know it was wrong. I'm sorry. I—" Naomi doesn't quite know how to treat the wound in their friendship. A laceration in dirty, still water. Perhaps nothing can be done. Was there anything her father or her mama could have done to receive her forgiveness? In her father's eyes, were there enough prayers, enough grit indentions on her knees, enough pleas to the Lord to be forgiven?

"I won't do it again. If I get a chance to not do it again. 'N I understand you love him 'n I won't say untrue things about him. 'N I'll try to keep the truth as kind as I can."

Clara doesn't respond right away. They both sit on the rocks wondering what to say and how to say it and if it will be enough. Sorry hadn't worked much in Naomi's experience. When aimed at God, there was never a rush of love like heroin to know she'd been pardoned. When aimed at her father, forgiveness took the shape of a belt. It was never verbally given, only physically paid for.

"We're not best friends again. Not yet." Clara looks at Naomi and her face relaxes. Anger slips from her expression like melted snow on a roof. "But I can't be too hard on you about it. Even the part where you snuck into my house. Because I was there, at your house, and I heard all the tapping. I know that wasn't… normal. But I also don't want you sugarcoating anything either. Don't be mean, don't be a liar, but don't be a bullshitter either. If there's some sort of ghost around here — even if you *claim* to have not seen it in a while — I'd rather not be dealing with it alone."

Naomi cracks a wry smile and uses her finger to cross her heart. "You're not. I promise," and Naomi means it. With her entire being. With every morning she's woken up regretting that Clara's not there beside her. She extends her hand to Clara and hoists her off the ground. "You got plans?"

"Not yet," Clara says.

"Wanna learn to fly fish?"

Naomi sits on the cool pebbles and sets up the rod and reel. She speaks as she goes through the steps. She places three fly options on her knee for Clara to choose from. She explains the advantages of each, and Clara points to one made of black fuzz and red sparkle. When finished, she demonstrates the act of casting.

Naomi points to riffles in the river that might be a good spot to cast towards. While the sky is no longer obscured by the greenery of the treetops, there are now brown stretch marks splitting across it from the bare branches. Places that, during the summer, will be full of leaves. However, in the spot they stand, not even empty branches mar their gaze toward the blue of the universe.

"I don't think I'll be able to hang out much," Clara says from her spot on a fallen log onshore. She tells Naomi that she isn't far along in her pregnancy. About two months. Right in the thick of her morning sickness. Naomi notes that Clara's conception date is close to when they stopped speaking, and guilt begins to gurgle in her gut.

"Havin' a baby's a big deal. I understand." Naomi tugs the line to ensure the fly darts along the bottom to seduce some unlucky fish.

"Yeah, kinda. Ethan's been pretty protective about the green bean since he found out." Clara takes a break from fishing to build a pile of stones. Her perimeter is dug out like a trench to find all the beautiful ones. A pyramid of white and beige and copper sits beside her. "Some people in town have told Ethan some shitty things about you. About your grandma and your dad. It really freaked Ethan out."

"I didn't hurt her," Naomi says of her Grandma Joyce. "But I won't pretend I like hardly any of 'em neither."

"Ethan said you have a brother in town." Naomi can hear the question in Clara's statement. *Why didn't you tell me? What are you hiding?*

"He's alright. We weren't close for a long time. That's only changed recently." Naomi wants to drop the subject, but considers Clara's request to not bullshit. Hiding in her own bullshit most likely counts. "I liked my other grandma. Dottie."

"The one with the letters?" Clara asks.

"Yeah. She married a bastard, but that seems to run in the family. But she tried, I think. Seemed sorrier than my mama, at least." Naomi continues to fish. Her heart is like an open book in the rain. Every word a droplet that will soak and tear the pages. So, she keeps fishing. Keeps the appearance of disinterest.

"What did your mom have to be sorry for?"

Silence drifts between them as Naomi's discomfort with being so open begins to take root. "Father wasn't a gentle man," she summarizes shortly.

Clara nods. "I know some of those." Naomi wants to segue into a discussion about Ethan but thinks better of it. It's too soon after declaring she won't be mean about her relationship with him. "My mom left my dad when I was little. I don't know much about it, but I know he made her think she was stupid. And she wasn't. She was the first in our family to get a degree. She studied art history. But she couldn't do much with it, so my dad made her feel bad about it.

"Nowadays, I feel guilty about moving from Kansas City. There, I had my mom and my aunts. If anything were to happen, I had people. People that would know what I'm going through."

"With the baby?" Naomi asks.

"If I left Ethan."

Naomi wants so badly to keep Clara on that line of thought. However, to keep the conversation heading down that path she knows she'll break her promise to not be mean. So, she tries to let it go as best as she can. "Dads are the worst," Naomi responds with uncertainty, but Clara laughs and her smile is good to see.

"Yeah, they are. Sorry about yours."

"Don't be. It's for the best he's dead." It's curt and honest.

"Oh. I meant that he was an asshole. I didn't know about that."

"Ah shit, yeah. Sorry. I didn't mean to be a dick about it." Naomi reels her line in and sinks the rod into the rocks. She plops down on the ground beside Clara. "I never liked him much. 'N I don't think he liked me either. Just the way I'm used to thinkin' about him, I guess."

"Was it anything bad?" And Naomi knows what she means. The stories of her father's tough love are ones she never dreamed of sharing. It's been ages since she fantasized about telling the police or a teacher about what waited for her at home. If she had, she wouldn't have been met by a social worker or new parents. It wasn't like the goofy old black and white police shows. Or the old cowboy movies she watched with her father. It would have meant more time in the cellar, more lashes with the belt.

In Naomi's experience with Erica, there wasn't a day that passed where the tales that danced on her tongue were so close to pirouetting off. But Clara trusts her enough to give her a taste of her father.

Naomi feels many things toward Clara: lust, love, friendship. But trust? Wasn't it trust that led Naomi to stay in the bathroom, playing patient, the day they met? And trust that led Clara into the *Davis* canoe this very day? Trust that's now allowing Naomi to watch Clara make her own choices? It's trust and respect, isn't it?

So, Naomi lets it all go. She spills her guts like a hog on the butcher's floor. Every gritty bit of truth and terror swirling the drain. All the blood from a childhood haunted by the looming presence of a God she never met and never felt, it all rushes out. She's consumed by the release. And when she's done, Clara places her hand on Naomi's and squeezes like she's trying to stop the blood. But this bloodletting of her memories is more cathartic than being nursed to health by Clara. Maybe that's for later.

"I'm so sorry," Clara finally says.

Naomi shrugs. It's better now, having said it, but still uncomfortable. "I'm sorry to dump that on you like that. You've got enough on your shoulders."

Clara withdraws her hand and tucks a few curls behind Naomi's ear. "Sometimes you gotta exchange what's on your shoulders with others. You take some of mine, I'll take some of yours."

Behind Clara and Naomi, trailing the canoe, is a stringer of brown trout. It'll be enough for a few dinners if she freezes them. Clara paddles and Naomi observes her shoulders push the water behind them. The muscles tensing and stretching with each stroke. Her hair falls down her back and between her shoulder blades. Clara's built muscle since moving to Blaire. Perhaps she continued going to the water even when they weren't together. There was quite a lot of missed time between the two. Naomi hopes Clara will fill her in on what she's missed.

Ryan meets the two at the put-in and assists them with hauling the canoe back to its lockup.

"I got it from here. Go home." Ryan smiles and shoos them away.

Naomi holds the rod in one hand and the tackle box in the other. In Clara's hands are a collection of river rocks she deems worthy of taking home. They rest in silence in the cab of the truck. The sun sets behind the trees in rays of gold and tangerine.

"If you want to hang out again, I think the best way is going to be at church. Ethan's worried about something happening to the baby. I'll be home most of the time except Wednesdays and Sundays. Blaire Baptist wanted someone to start fixing up the community garden, so I volunteered." Clara holds her hands in her lap. Her eyelashes flicker as she gazes upon the winter road ahead.

Naomi's visit to the church in August was her first time stepping foot within a hundred yards of it in over a decade. She half expected to burst into flames when she entered the supposedly holy ground. However, with Clara nearly on house arrest, she finds herself closer to agreeing than she ever thought possible. Her father isn't there. Her mama, her brother, sure. But if Naomi is leaving soon, maybe saying one last goodbye won't be so terrible.

Spring

Chapter Twenty-One

Naomi skips the first Sunday service after Clara invites her. For days, she desperately tries to conjure even one decent memory from within that church. And for days, all she remembers is every horribly toxic parenting choice brought on by religious paranoia, generational trauma, and sadism. It's all stuck in her throat and grows more difficult to dislodge.

For three days, she smokes like a chimney. Naomi hasn't done that since Erica died. Back then, she nearly bathed in Erica's vanilla body spray and filled her house with weed smoke so that every breath she took was like Erica was right there and would always be right there.

But weed can't soothe Naomi this time. With each puff, her paranoia grows. Although it's been weeks since she's seen a haint, that suddenly offers very little relief to her. She lived thirty years of her life without knowing it existed. Then it emerged like a corpse from a grave to terrorize her and wreak havoc on her budding relationships. A few weeks of its absence doesn't mean it's gone entirely.

Naomi rests on her couch, fire roaring, and her third joint of the hour rests between her middle and index fingers. Her hands shake throughout the day, her chest and stomach ache. The kettle is on the stove so she can brew a cup of tea in hopes that it will shoo away whatever ailment has crawled into her lungs.

Naomi read all of the Curtis family's book on herbalism. It cites peppermint as helpful for chest pain and dandelion for the stomach. And Great-Grandma Opa's handwriting — Naomi has studied the book enough that she has identified each family member's scrawl — confirms the finding with a black-ink star beside the heading. The hot drink fills her from toe to tongue, but it doesn't relieve the weight that rests on top of her.

Much of the information within the herbalism manuscript is a bit above Naomi's gardening education. Many of the plants she's never even heard of. Even with the black and gray sketches of their leaves and flowers. Within the margins, she discovers minute details about her family members, like how much Great-Aunt Eda liked purple flowers — she circled each one. How many plants that assist with pain management were underlined in blue ink, which was most often used by Great-Grandpa Walter. How Great-Aunt Petunia's handwriting wasn't as pretty as her sister's, but she wrote the most Bible charms in the encyclopedia.

The God that they write about is so different from the God her father taught her to fear. Although it's still not her cup of tea, she finds this version gentler and more comforting. A God she can see some type of relationship with. *But not now,* she knows.

Naomi still debates whether she'll meet Clara at church at all. It's Saturday again, and her decision bares down on her like dirt being thrown down scoop by scoop as she lies paralyzed in an open coffin. *Fuck, is this what Father felt like?* She hopes so, but there is also a swirl of strange pity for him.

Her chest grows heavier with the thought. Each breath takes added effort to suck in and force out. Her fingers reek of skunky haze and her ashtray nearly overflowing. A mental image of her tiptoeing to the trash as it wisps away into the air, onto her sweater, all over the floor, overtakes her mind. *It'll make a goddamn mess. Such a mess. A mess.* Each breath is shorter than the last.

What will her first sermon be when she goes back to her old prison? They won't expect her the first time. But the second? Surely it will be directed at her. Something less forgiving. Naomi can feel herself sitting in those uncomfortable antique pews. The nails on her smaller toes digging into each other inside her too-small Mary Janes. The bows in her hair scratching at her neck. Her dress crushing her breasts and constricting her like a boa.

Suddenly, she's in the church again. Each pew holds people sitting black-padded shoulder to black-padded shoulder cramped together. The air is heavy with the stench of smoke and hairspray and sweat. In perfect synchronicity, she watches the churchgoers turn to face her, their movements smooth. Their heads rotate like barn owls, with their shoulders still facing forward.

Each set of eyes is a verdant blaze, driving into her deeper than the stitches on her dress or the ache in her chest. A hundred solar eclipses are aimed at her, and she can't look away as their luminosity increases and green eyes become lighthouse beacons calling her forward. Synchronized mouths begin to open as if to yell at her "leave," "get out," and "you'll never be welcome here again," but they say nothing. Each set of jaws cracks open further and further until a thousand caves are aimed at her, larger than the head of the person. Their lips stretch wide. A high-pitched whistling scream erupts from the mouths like a death siren: an omen.

Naomi's breaths are gasps. Her chest has a boulder on top of it, her sternum caving in and her heart is close to being exposed and crushed. Sweat slicks between her shoulder blades and under her arms. She lifts them to give her torso more space to expand and to keep her sweaty arms from touching anything. The wetness is an electric shock each time it touches.

Naomi springs to her feet and sprints to the front door. The screaming follows her. She runs down her icy steps and into the snowy yard. She doesn't notice the burn of ice on her bare feet or legs. After a couple of yards, she falls to her knees. Each strangled puff of air carries no oxygen to her lungs or brain. Just old dusty smoke and hairspray and sweat. Naomi collapses to all fours and buries her face in the snow.

A pink fleshy haze can be seen through the skin of her eyelids. She holds her breath until she can't any longer and she pulls herself back to her knees. She keeps her face in the frigid March air for only a second before she plunges herself back into a fresh patch of snow and stays until she's desperate for oxygen again. Naomi repeats this several times until she begins to sense that her knees burn as if they are on hot coals and not snow. Until the break between each breath and plunge no longer squeezes like a man sitting on top of her.

One last time, she forces herself into a kneeling prayer position and looks out across the yard. A snowfall has begun. Glittering, twinkling formations of crystalized ice drift across the gray sky and tree branches that streak like brown oaken lightning across the horizon. The flakes are large and float rather than fall. Like they dance all the way from the heavens to earth.

Through the field of snowfall, Naomi sees the pawpaw tree. It's bare of leaves and sweet fruit. Its yellowed leaves have long since fallen and been swept away by wind and weather and rake. On the thin branches of the pawpaw, Naomi spots the beginnings of buds like tiny buttons sprinkled through the tree.

Flitting around the barren branches of the pawpaw are swallowtail butterflies. The black tips of their wings drew her eye against the white haze of snowfall. At least a dozen of them circle and swarm the tree like children around a bonfire. Although the snow collects on Naomi's eyelashes and her legs burn like glacial hellfire, spring draws closer.

The following Wednesday morning, Naomi sits in the comfort of her heated truck for a few minutes longer. It's the only vehicle in the lot. The absence of cars leads her to believe no one's here.

She knows it will be Aaron up at the front when she eventually shows up for a Sunday service. With a face too similar to their father's, with the eyes of their mama. Maybe now, he's put on that woolen suit and tie, holds their father's briefcase, and has climbed those stairs to the podium that puts him closer to the heavens than the rest of his congregation.

Then Clara's head pops up over the brambles of the garden. Her hair is pulled into a braid and a beanie covers her ears, matching her hair. She looks as though she was birthed by the earth itself. Naomi finally gets out of the car to go to her.

"Glad you're here," Clara smiles. "Can you grab me that basket over there?" She points a gloved finger to the entrance by Naomi's feet. "I'm pulling out all the annuals. Whoever did this last year used popsicle sticks to mark the plants. Makes it easy."

"What's an annual?" Naomi hands Clara the woven basket and kneels.

"Plants that only live one growing season, then don't come back." Clara wraps her hand around the base of a plant and pulls it, roots-and-all, from its resting spot. She drops it in the basket. "Can you pull up the cucumbers in the corner?"

Naomi shuffles on denim knees to the cucumbers. The garden is large, with three rectangular raised beds. In between each row and column are walkways. The paths are made of packed down grass, like deer trails, lined with stacked two-by-fours that create the barrier of the beds. The corpses of cucumber vines slither up three poles connected by the same chicken wire that lines the perimeter of the garden.

Naomi didn't bring gloves, but she enjoys the cool air on her skin and the tough tug of coarse and brittle vines as she jerks the roots out of the soil. Starting at the top of the poles and chicken wire, Naomi unlaces the vines and tosses them into the basket. The two women work in silence, occasionally requesting shears from the other, or Clara sometimes giving Naomi a new task.

Cleaning out the garden here seems different than the one at home. Like it's less destructive here with Clara.

She knows how to rip all this out in order for there to be a nice clear new place to grow, Naomi thinks.

The sun is just above the horizon when they begin, and directly overhead when they call it quits for the day. All of the annuals have been plucked and chucked. Their old resting spots were combed for leftover roots and rocks. The popsicle sticks marking their old homes remain as a reminder of what will be planted in the new season.

"We can start seeds on Sunday if you're coming." Clara bats soil off of her gloves and plucks the fabric off finger by finger before tucking them into the back of her jeans. There's a dusting of dirt across her nose and cheeks. Like earthy freckles.

"Who all helps?" Naomi asks.

"Just me. They might think it's odd if you don't attend service though." Clara begins to walk toward the church.

Naomi blurts out, "Yeah, can't let 'em know about my crush on you."

Clara snorts and then tilts her head to the side. "Hey, Naomi?"

Oh, I fucked up, Naomi screams at herself. "Mmhmm?"

"I don't mean to be rude, and you don't have to say anything—" Clara starts.

I fucked up.

"But are you gay? It's just, you've never mentioned a boyfriend, but you did talk to me for an hour once about your favorite nineties actresses."

Naomi holds her breath for a moment of shame, then lets it go. "Uh, yep."

Clara smiles and starts toward the church again. "Cool. Thanks for telling me. I assume Blaire isn't a great place for finding a girlfriend."

"Not in my experience," Naomi quips. Her eyes remain on the golden woman in front of her. For months, the thought of this conversation about her sexuality was horrifying. Her entire life, really. With the exception of one smoke session with Erica. Yet here she stands on the other side of it, Clara still with her.

The oversized white doors of the church open and reveal the ancient hickory floors and matching pews. Naomi is consumed by emptiness. This place, which supposedly represents eternal and unconditional love to so many countless people over thousands of years, is hollow around her. It's never been an ornate church. Baptists don't believe in decorating with crucifixes and depictions of a dying son of God.

At the time of the building's re-creation, the windows were custom-made in St. Louis. They're larger than any others in the town. Although the church looks to be nothing special in comparison to the wonders of the world, it's Blaire's own wonder. The only one it has besides the Kemiwe and the beautiful mountains and hollers it's built on. Those windows and the handcrafted pews and floors, sanded and stained by the town's ancestors, are a relic of adoration and devotion that will outlast every member of the congregation.

"It is kinda pretty," Naomi whispers. Clara walks to the front, past the podium. There's an ivory door that leads to a storage room containing a refrigerator, among other things.

Naomi remembers it all. Clara emerges with a sandwich in each hand. The pair sit in the back pew and eat.

"Thanks for coming," Clara says between bites.

"Sorry, I skipped last week."

"It's alright."

Naomi ponders how this whole opening-up thing works. She knows it's necessary work to be done in an effort towards recuperating their friendship. *But is there a proper way to start it? When I told her about Father at the river, does that mean I can keep confessing?* She just isn't like Clara in that regard. So willing to be open with another.

"How's the baby?"

"Fine." Clara continues to eat. Naomi gives her peace to continue. "I don't really know. The doctor says it's alright. I don't really have a connection to it yet, though. I don't really know when that's supposed to happen."

"There's plenty of time," Naomi tries to comfort her as best as she can.

"Until there's not." Clara places the sandwich down on her lap. "I didn't want one," she concedes. "I did my best to not let it happen. I stopped it once. Before we moved."

Naomi decides it's best not to speak yet. She gives Clara all the open air she needs to breathe and tell her story.

"I probably shouldn't be sayin' this in a church, but I've been on birth control since I was sixteen. We use condoms. Few months before we left Kansas City, I found out I was pregnant. Went to a clinic and they confirmed it. It fucking sucked. Birth control sucks. Condoms suck. And it still didn't fucking work. I didn't really know how to go about taking care of it. Couldn't tell Ethan or my mom. So, I went to the top of the stairs in our place, put my arms over my head, and fell."

Silence envelopes them like a dark, cold cave. Their fingers touch on the seat between them and spark a comforting fire that Naomi hopes keeps Clara warm, too.

"Of course, like a month after that, I found out they make pills that do the same job. I could have ordered them online. They're real secretive about it. Would've saved me a trip to the ER and a set of stitches." Clara lifts her fingers from their bonfire-touch to her chin. A thin pale line a few shades lighter than her skin with dots in pairs where the stitches pierced her skin.

Naomi noted the scar the first time she saw Clara. Although, it was her lovely red dress and gentle hands that ended up stealing Naomi's thoughts that day. *And the haint*, growls a part of her mind that she wishes would hush.

"I don't know how it happened again."

"Are you gonna do somethin' about it this time?" Naomi asks.

"The stairs weren't all that safe the first time. And I'm too far along for those abortion pills. I thought I'd just been having light periods for a while. I was real fucking wrong about that." Clara chuckles, but there isn't any joy in her laughter or her eyes. "But what's done is done."

Naomi sucks in a breath. "You think he'll be a good dad?" She bites her tongue as she recalls her promise to Clara: *"Don't be mean, don't be a liar, but don't be a bullshitter."* The comment seems mean, but it certainly isn't fertilized by bullshit either.

"I don't know. I certainly hope he relaxes. He keeps bringing up the fall and helping me with every damn flight of stairs. I'm sick of it already. And I've got six more months of this shit."

Uncertainty fills Naomi. She doesn't want to be another person coddling Clara like a naive child. Her friend isn't a glass ornament to be placed on a shelf and only visited to dust off what time has collected. Clara works with her knees and hands in the dirt during every season of the year. She learned to swim in her adulthood in river waters that have been known to wash people away. She chanced death — or at least serious harm and public damnation — to ensure her own autonomy in a state that won't guarantee it for her.

What does a person say to a woman like that? What does a woman like that need?

"I'll be here," Naomi offers. "In town, I mean. So, you've got somebody who'll let you go down the stairs by your own damn self."

Clara's laugh comes out with sniffles. "I'll be alright if you aren't."

"I know. But I kinda wanna stick around. The leaves'll be comin' in soon anyhow. No sense leavin' in the spring. Or the summer." Naomi gazes out the window. The forest of empty trees wavers in the breeze. Soon it will be lush and lively and the sorrow that fills Naomi every winter will lighten.

I'd like to see that again.

"I don't think I'll be much fun on Sundays when I come by," Naomi admits.

"You don't have to be fun all the time."

"My grandpa generations back built this place. First one burnt down over a hundred years ago. There's been a Darby reverend since the first."

"I'd kill to have these floors in my house," Clara jokes.

"He didn't do none of that. None of the pretty stuff inside. Just the buildin' itself. Other church folks gave the lumber and sanded and stained it real nice." Naomi swipes her hand along the oak wood of the pew. She considers how many sermons they've been present for. "I used to think my ass was gonna be flat as my grandma's if I kept sittin' on this damn thing."

Naomi waits for the next part to be easier, but it won't happen on its own. The words keep getting stuck halfway out of her throat. "I hate this place. Nothin' good ever happened for me here. Maybe with Father gone, it'll be better. But God tastes bad even now. I'm not gonna be fun while I'm in here. It'll be better when we're outside."

Clara covers Naomi's hand with her own. "I don't know if I'll be able to sit next to you. Maybe sometimes. But I'll sit where we can see each other. Alright? And I'll blink twice to tell you that everything is okay."

Chapter Twenty-Two

The woven basket that lives in the community garden rests in the crook of Naomi's arm as she works. She kneels in the dirt pretending to busy herself with this or that as folks mosey out of Sunday service and into their parked cars. Clara emerges with Ethan close behind, one hand on her lower back and the other holding her bicep as she walks down the stairs with ease.

Clara sits down on the earth beside her, Sunday dress crushed between herself and the wet earth. "We'll be working inside today, starting seeds."

"Is it alright if we wait out here 'til everybody's gone?"

"Sure." The two wait, dirty in their garden. The snow from a few days earlier has mostly melted. Temperature is a fickle thing in Missouri. It skates back and forth between cold and windy and temperate and wet.

"As I live and breathe, Miss Naomi Darby." A familiar and boisterous voice announces over the empty churchyard.

Above the tangle of dormant plants, Aaron's head bobbles as he walks over the uneven ground toward them. "What's got you diggin' in the weeds out here with our newest congregant?"

Aaron oozes the same ill-fitting confidence her father wore day in and day out. It seems as though no one ever noticed — with her brother or her father — that this patched suit of morale is made of the cheapest fabric.

It doesn't suit Aaron. "I've been wantin' to learn to garden. She's teachin' me."

His hands are as large as their father's as they rest on his hips. His black suit and matching tie contrast against his ivory button-up and polished shoes that shine like silver. His smile does too, but closer to fool's gold. "Well, we do appreciate the work you two are puttin' in. Lookin' forward to another bountiful harvest!"

"It's fun to work on something that so many people will get to enjoy. Something for the community," chirps Clara. "I'm sorry, by the way. To both of you, for what happened to your grandma."

"Sorry, I didn't go to her service. I thought it best not to. Didn't wanna upset nobody by bein' there." Naomi's eyes hold Aaron's. She wants him to know how sincerely she means it.

"Your appearance wouldn't ever upset nobody. You're a Darby. This church is as much yours as anybody in Blaire." He turns on his heel towards the lot. "I look forward to seein' you next week, sister! Oh, and Clara? Storage room is unlocked. Seeds and soil are beneath the table."

Aaron's sticky insincerity doesn't go unnoticed by Naomi. How differently he seems to behave when others are around. Like his position as reverend is a performance. *Or he's new to it and nervous*, she chides.

Once inside the storage room, the first thing Naomi notices are several stacks of charcoal and propane tanks.

"What's all this for?"

"Donations for the spring barbeque in a few weeks," Clara says as she prepares the seeding supplies.

Naomi scrunches her eyebrows in confusion. "We never did a spring barbeque."

Her companion shrugs. "Aaron brought it up a few weeks ago as a way to start his tenure as reverend. Ethan may be a pain in the ass, but the man was born and raised in Kansas City and his brisket is amazing!"

Clara places plastic grocery store produce containers on the table. She lines the seed packets up in front of them and asks Naomi to pass her the painter's tape from under a fold-out table. With a thick marker, Clara writes the name of each type of seed and sticks labeled tape on the coordinating plastic nursery. Naomi cuts the corner off the bag of soil and begins pouring the dirt into each container until full.

They start on opposite sides of the table, delicately placing seeds and covering them ever so slightly with soil. Clara uses a spray bottle to coat them with water. The sun from the window will eventually coax each seedling from its hut and into the world.

"You don't have to come on Sundays. I'll be alright. At least Wednesdays there's nobody here. You don't have to deal with all this," Clara waves her hands in a gesture to the church.

Naomi smiles roguishly. "I don't mind it. That wasn't the part I hated. Aaron's completely full of it, but he's

alright. The worst is over so I'm alright comin' on Sundays."
Naomi pauses. "I ain't gonna throw a party or nothin'
though."

March flows into April and then May. Each month
builds to create a current of seasons, like ripples in the river.
The church seed sprouts burst through the soil in the
backroom, and a few weeks later, Clara and Naomi plant
each infant under the sky and watch them reach for the sun.
The foliage of the garden seems to grow inches by the day.
The warmth of spring is upon the small town, with
righteous rainstorms every week to alleviate the early waves
of heat.

Every Wednesday, Naomi drives back home to her own
garden and copies what Clara taught her that day. The fence
is now painted blue as the spring sky. She finds solitude in
her garden. Each day there's something to be done. She
waters and fertilizes and trims. In all her years in Grandma
Dottie's house, Naomi never imagined that the garden
could be as giving and beautiful as it was for its previous
caretaker. Before Clara, Naomi thought that all gardening
could possibly be was burying seeds in dirt and watering.
Now, she tests the pH balance of the soil and fertilizes at
regular intervals.

Alongside the education that Clara provides, Naomi
reads through her family's hidden encyclopedia. She works
on memorizing each annotation and native crop to the area.
The old family Bible rests on her empty bookshelf. Its
presence doesn't taunt or aggravate her. It's a relic of family
history to be acknowledged and learned from, but not
obeyed.

Clara's belly is round enough now to easily imagine the little person inside. Although Naomi does her best to remain neutral toward the outcome of Clara's pregnancy, she finds herself growing excited about the prospects. There will be birthday parties and Christmases to look forward to. Tiny shoes and sweaters come fall. Toes in green grass after that.

Naomi imagines introducing the baby to the Kemiwe. She will teach them all the beauty there is to find in these hills. How to fish and swim and forage. That there are forsaken aspects of life, but their mama is *good*. Never mind their father. Maybe one day Clara will have a mind to leave him, realize that he's no good for her.

The three of them — Clara, baby, and Naomi — could live together in Grandma Dottie's house now that the place is clean and fixed up. Clara will paint the walls in beautiful colors and Naomi will crochet baby blankets. Pictures of their family will line the halls and toys will be scattered across the floor.

Naomi wants to keep them safe so badly. There is beauty in these hills but there is evil, too. These woods hold its cruelty so tightly and for so long. As if their decimation in the centuries before left the evil with nowhere to hide. It holds fast to its heartache and rage and betrayal.

Another spring Sunday brings Naomi to Blaire Baptist. When she finds the lot empty, she immediately knows where to look next. A dramatic sigh fills the cab of her truck, and she keeps on the road until she reaches the next left turn. Once spring and summer roll around, when swimming is possible, Sunday service is often held at the swimming hole off the main road. It's a rounded curve in

the Kemiwe that has been used for baptisms for as long as
Blaire Baptist has existed.

The tunnel of leaves has enveloped the road again and
the turtles and frogs are back to their warm-weather ways of
making the gravel street their burial ground. The road is
lined with over half the cars in Blaire. Most are trucks and
decades-old sedans. There is mismatched paint on side
doors or hoods, highlighting vehicles that persevered
through financial crises and years of repairs.

Naomi arrives as close to the start of service as she can.
She hopes to be the last to arrive. Her panic-induced
nightmare surfaces in her memory. Their illuminated eyes
like the sun through river water and their jaws opening wide
like cave mouths. But these are just people. *Just assholes.*

Naomi dismisses tradition and habit. Her Sunday best
still hangs in her closet, and she's dressed in clothes to
garden in: jeans and a t-shirt. Aaron stands under a hickory
tree at the top of the slope above the river. He's dressed
down in comparison to what she expects: dress shoes and
slacks with a button-down rolled to the elbow. His flock
form a half-circle in front of him as they sing a hymn
Naomi has long since forgotten.

It allows her mind to wander, and her eyes follow suit
over the tops of heads and shoulders in search of Clara. A
few rows ahead is an amber halo of hair. As if she senses
Naomi's eyes, she turns ever so slightly, and they smile at
one another. Clara blinks twice and Naomi settles into the
sand.

As the singing ends, Aaron begins to preach.

"Today is the start of something new. Now I know we
don't make habit of hootin 'n hollerin' about new things.
We like it classic and comfortable." Aaron's met with

laughter and muted cheers. "However, the Lord gives us new gifts every day. 'N this day our gift is new life — youth — to our congregation. My father was a reverend here for over twenty years. Many folks here today remember his father before him preachin' each 'n every week. Over time, Blaire adjusted and grew to respect my father the same as his father before him. I hope to give you reason to do the same for me. However, in order for that to happen, there are grievances that must be aired."

Murmurs erupt through the crowd. Naomi's heart soars. Her pride acts as helium as she observes her little brother take on their small world.

"I have learned much about my family in the past few months. I have learned about our history right here—" Aaron stomps his foot in the soft sand, "—in Blaire. My father—" he pauses. He huffs. Then he raises his head and looks at his followers head-on. "My father loved you all. He did. And his father before him, too. They loved you as He loves you. But their practice wasn't without fault. We must all believe that there is eternally space to grow. We can always rise higher! We must. For God is everywhere, but for us to be with Him at our end we must rise to Him. He will not meet us in the mud. He is not dirty as we are."

"Amen!" A man near the front hollers. A chorus of copies follows. The balloon within Naomi begins to deflate. Horror, and worst of all, *disappointment* take its place.

"My father was not a perfect man. But he was a good one. He did what he believed was best for this congregation, for his *family*." The word stings worse than any bee or glass to the palm. "We must take his legacy — *my* legacy — and build upon it with marble and gold and we will rise higher than ever. We will be free at last." Aaron's arms are wide in a gesture to welcome all those in front of him into his open arms.

Half an hour later, Aaron leads several members down to the river. He wades in up to his waist and gestures for the first of those to be baptized. A line of small children forms, and the first steps forward. She can't be any older than eight. Not much older than Naomi was at her own baptism. The girl's long blue dress floats in the water as she walks in. A hard shiver rocks her small frame and Aaron clasps her hand. Naomi's heart continues to break. The manipulative act of coercing children to give themselves to something they don't understand — to put them in that still-icy water when they are just babies — it follows her as she walks to her truck.

Naomi remembers what those children feel. She was only six at the one time she experienced what the others call *God*. As the reverend's daughter, she was in Bible study from the moment she got home from school. Psalms were read, hymns were sung, and they were all kept up until the early morning hours of the next day each Wednesday night.

She remembers her father shouting and the others following his lead. It's hazy, the memory. Naomi can't say what was being read or what the sermon was that day. But she recalls the white-hot light that shot through her. The crack that split her mind and the tears that ran down her cheeks. Suddenly, her shoes no longer hurt her feet and her dress no longer felt tight. Her voice ripped through the chorus of shouts and singing and amens and hallelujahs. Naomi's feet were lifted off the ground and she felt as though she were flying above them all. As though she was the closest of all of them to God.

Slowly, her eyes peeked open and she saw the wood paneling of the church ceiling. Hands of other parishioners on her back, holding her up above them. Naomi's eyes scanned down from where she knew the steeple stood on the roof, down past the wall behind the podium, until she reached her father's eyes. They glowed with pride. Their usual black fury burned gold. His mouth opened wide as he yelled something she could not hear. His brow dripped in sweat and the skin was taut across his knuckles. When he stopped chanting, his mouth twisted into a huge and gruesome smile, followed by tears that stained his cheeks.

Naomi was slowly placed back on her feet, and she collapsed. The thuds of her father's heavy footsteps down the stairs from his platform where he stood above them all echoed in her ears. His large hands scooped her up and into his arms. "My daughter has felt the Lord."

Hallelujah! They all joined. And the next day, the two walked together to the river and he carefully dipped her in the Kemiwe, and the water washed over her face. Naomi opened her eyes while she was under and gazed at her father. His form waved and shimmered through the water. The sky was blue and beautiful and the water warm and inviting.

Neither God nor her father ever felt the same as that night when she was lifted above them all. As she grew older, she learned that it was a technique that the Southern Baptist Church specialized in. They often exhaust their congregants to the point of near hysteria to induce an emotional response. To induce something that might feel like God. Naomi swears she will never fall for that kind of trick again.

What the fuck happened? Aaron talks and talks and *talks* but he doesn't say anything real. He speaks like a low-level manager making a dollar over what his employees earn. His words mean nothing. They are pretty and likely exactly what folks want to hear. He speaks of doing better, improving, but nothing of why or how. Nothing of what he discussed with Naomi. *Didn't he promise me? Didn't he say he would change it?*

Sitting in the garden with vines that grow taller than her head, Naomi hides from the day. Clara will arrive soon, and Naomi will be free to pour her heart out about her frustration with her brother. She knows Clara will listen and give comfort and advice like wine. But every second is an eternity.

The grinding of tires on gravel wrenches her from her ruminations as Aaron's and the marshal's vehicles pull into the lot. They park side by side. Aaron jumps out and jogs inside. Ethan leans against his door and lights a cigarette. *I bet you only do that when Clara's not around*, and Naomi knows it's true. When Aaron reemerges, he's wearing jeans and has two beers in hand.

"Care for one?" Aaron offers.

"Thanks. One of my favorite vices." Ethan's voice is cheerful. "And what's your vice, Reverend?" The marshal pokes at the man.

"Oh, I suppose I like to learn about folks," he offers with a swig. "And a good glass of whisky."

The marshal guffaws, "Load of horse shit, *Reverend.*"

Aaron's face grows more serious. "It's necessary for important men like us to know what the goin's on of town are. Wouldn't you agree, Marshal?"

The shorter man nods. "I suppose so."

The wicked smile returns to her brother's face. "Speakin' of which, you weren't at the river today." He looks like the cat that caught the canary.

"Well, I was wantin' to apologize for that—" Ethan starts.

"Oh, that's alright. You're a man of God and the law. You must make time for 'em both." The hand that doesn't grip the beer is stuck in his pocket as if he hasn't a care in the world.

The two men laugh. "Thanks for understandin'. I got in a bit of trouble with my last position. Felt like I was expected to be everywhere at once, you know? This right here —" Ethan shakes his beer bottle. "Is the exact thing they wouldn't tolerate."

"We have hard jobs, Marshal. Somethin's gotta give. So, what did you need to talk about so bad?"

Ethan pulls sighs and twirls his mustache as he thinks. "Coroner officially ruled your granny's death an accident."

Naomi has a lightness in her that she hasn't felt since the day her Grandma Joyce died. While she did *know* that she didn't push her own blood down those stairs, and even her brother told her that the marshal no longer suspected her, it is the greatest of reliefs to hear it from the horse's mouth. As if maybe there is truth to it if the law believed it. But it's settled; the paperwork is signed. She is as good as innocent.

"And what exactly about that situation made them think that?" Aaron's voice is bewildered. It's the confirmation of

Naomi's fear since the accident: her brother does believe she killed Grandma Joyce.

"No sign of a struggle. That calcium issue I told you 'bout. Brittle bones break. And that she was havin' difficulty walkin' from her previous fracture. A fall down — how many stairs are out at Naomi's place? Ten or so? Well anyway, that'll do it. Although it ain't what *I* believe, knowin' your sister, but the forensics ain't on our side. They said her heel likely broke and that's what made her tumble. The color of her heel matches what was left on a scratch on the porch." Ethan wipes his brow of sweat with the cold bottle.

"Damn. And she's just gonna get away with it?"

"Not much we can do this time. But she'll slip up again. Hell, we get her with a warrant for drug possession — maybe sellin' if we really wanna throw the book at her — and she'll be put up for a while," Ethan consoles Aaron. "Reckon if you take a drive out there and see something white and powdery you call us, Reverend. We could get that warrant ready lickety-split."

"Reckon I might take you up on that." Aaron wears a wry smile. At that moment he looks more like their father than ever before. Naomi is sick. "Hmm. Anythin' I can do to pay you back for your tireless work, Marshal?"

Ethan switches his weight to his other leg nervously. "Hell, maybe you can forgive me a few transgressions and we can make it even."

Aaron belly laughs. "We ain't Catholic, Ethan! We don't have a damn box in there to sit in and tell me all your sins." Then he pauses and leans toward the wiry officer. "But if you wanna tell me for shits and giggles, then I'd be real interested."

The pair push closer together like children on the playground telling secrets. "My wife's been a bit... difficult lately. Whole lotta headaches. I just can't get her to roll over. So, the other night she's at it again: 'Not now, baby, my head hurts, my back hurts,' blah blah blah," Ethan quotes Clara in a condescending baby voice. "And I say to her, 'Aw baby let me fix that. The good Lord gave me the best medicine right here,'" he grabs his crotch. Aaron chuckles. "Anyway, I did feel a little bad after."

Aaron interrupts him with a hand. "It is your wife's duty to assist her husband. Ain't nothin' to feel bad about. She's your wife. You ain't takin' anythin' that's not already yours. Nothin' to forgive."

In one swift motion, all hope — all *faith* — that Naomi had in her brother vanishes. The years — *the decade* — she spent in these hills alone thinking maybe one day he will see what she saw in their parents and the church slips away. *It was all a waste.* There is no fixing what he's said. The green-light he's given to the sole marshal of Blaire to comfort him after he committed a crime — a sin. Naomi wasted away in that empty house by herself for so long with no friends and no family. Waiting for a man who's chosen the same path as their father.

"Now you wanna talk about nasty. I heard tell that a certain pregnancy in town wasn't exactly an accident." Aaron's voice is poison in Naomi's heart.

Please don't be Clara. Please don't be Clara, Naomi thinks.

"Now who in Sam Hill told you that? It was that damn bartender at *Stokes*, wasn't it?" Ethan smiles despite being caught doing something so heinous. "Well, I have been pokin' holes in all her plans if you know what I mean. But the good ol' state of Missouri doesn't let pregnant women divorce."

As the marshal closes his eyes in laughter, the reverend keeps his wide open and Naomi sees the shift. Their deep brown color — a shade unidentifiable from the distance Naomi is at but she knows by heart — gleams green. As if a flashlight has been projected through lime paper. A glow that could attract moths. A glow Naomi has seen many times in the past several months, dwelling at the bottom of the river or floating in the woods, or attached to a black shadow creature or an old woman taller than any person she's ever seen.

Everything has changed so quickly. Naomi's beloved brother, crushed to dust in minutes. But something must be done.

Chapter Twenty-Three

Soon the two men quit their locker room talk and the marshal jumps back into his SUV. Dust rolls after him as he takes a left toward town. Aaron heads back inside the church for around thirty minutes or so before he emerges with a beaten brown leather case. The case is a familiar sight to the Darby family. It was their father's. The old man used it to store his notes for sermons, as well as to protect his generations-old family Bible during travel.

Eddie told his children that it was a gift to their great-great-great grandfather from his brother. Inside the front cover is an ink inscription dated 1889 from Savannah, Georgia. They were told the book had seen the fall of the great Ozark forest and its rebirth from the fallen stone of the eroded mountains. So much had happened to the land and its people in those hundred and fifty years. It was an entirely new place in so many ways. Not even the same types of trees grow in abundance here anymore. Yet somehow this old book remains.

Naomi listens to Aaron's footfalls on the church lot as he approaches his car. The heirloom briefcase is tucked at the feet of the passenger side, and he slides his keys into the ignition before he clicks his seatbelt into place. This is Naomi's signal to unleash hell.

She crashes his nearly empty whisky bottle against his right temple. He pulls his hands up to shield himself far too late. A few shards poke through his skin and the other side of his head ricochets off of the window.

Aaron tries to turn around, but his move is too sudden and the seatbelt resists. Fingers fumble to unlock himself, but Naomi wraps a thin rope over his head and pulls it tight against his throat. He immediately relinquishes his attempt to unbuckle himself and desperately grasps at the rope strangling him. His struggle is useless. He reaches his arm back and grabs a handful of her curls. He yanks as hard as he can from the uncomfortable angle, but Naomi just pulls the rope tighter. Forcing him to choose between hurting her and saving himself.

She looks up to the rearview mirror to see him staring at her, his eyes bugging out of their sockets. To his left, his desperate fingers find the seat release and the back leans out until it hits Naomi's knees. Aaron tries to use the small amount of time that the rope slackens to release himself, but she wastes no time and bludgeons him in the eye with her hand.

"Naomi—" he yells but she cracks the side of her fist into his eye again. His hands quickly come up to block another hit, but she moves over the center console and onto Aaron's lap. The seat belt is still latched over his waist so he tries again to unlock it, but Naomi hits him again and again until she thinks his right eye might not be intact anymore.

"The power of Christ compels you!" Naomi shouts at the man she once called brother. It's a laughable play and likely only something that is done in the movies. She places her knee on top of the seat belt lock to prevent him from unfastening himself. Both of his eyes are closed, and he holds one hand to his damaged right eye and the other in front of him to block Naomi's fists.

Aaron's laugh leaks from him like toxic gas. It fuels her anger, and she brings her fist down again, this time on his left eye.

"Won't work if there is no God. And even if there is, you left Him long ago." He grabs her right wrist and wrenches it down between his seat and the door. "Look at me, Naomi."

Face to face, only inches away, she sees his muscles twitch by his left eye and before he can open it, she bites down as hard as she can on his shoulder through his shirt. Aaron roars and relinquishes her wrist before he shoves her hard into the steering wheel, releasing a honk into the empty parking lot.

Before Aaron can touch the wound on his shoulder, Naomi lurches forward and forces her thumbs into both of his eye sockets. She screams and her voice breaks. Blood and tears gather in the sunken sockets of her brother's eyes. Red rivers flow in thick tracks down his cheeks. Tributaries stream across to his temples and into Naomi's clenched palms as they hold tight to the sides of his head to ensure her grip and the complete destruction of his eyes.

Aaron's cries are incredibly human. Too human. As if they are imitations of a human, like when a cougar cries. So abnormally real. He grabs her wrists and squeezes as tight as he can and her hands release. Naomi falls back against the horn, but if it sounds, she can't hear it over the screams and the rush of blood in her ears. His howls continue as he cradles his beaten face and blood leaks from between his fingers as he tries to sit up.

Naomi fumbles for the door handle and abruptly falls to the gravel onto her shoulder. She drags herself a few feet away before rising to her feet. Scouring the woods nearest to the scene, she finds a branch and drags it back to where Aaron weeps.

Bloody fingers feel for his seatbelt one last time. It clicks and he tries for the door to find it already open. He falls to his stomach on the ground and pulls himself to his knees. "Naomi why? What are you doin'?" He cries. "Please stop. Please. I'm your brother. Please."

"Liar."

The rough bark of the branch rips at his face as she bashes him on the side of the head. Blood flies from his mouth and, as he lays motionless in the gravel, it leaks into a pool beside him. His fake, *pathetic* cries finally stop. Naomi needs to move fast.

Aaron's back rises and falls with each breath. It's only a matter of time until he's able to fight back again. She races to the trunk. While the reverend was inside, she'd found a bundle of twine in the church's garden as well as a burlap grow bag.

Naomi wraps his wrists over and over in twine. Next, his ankles. She yanks the bag over his face and more twine is added around his throat to ensure that the bag won't be removed. Aaron is of average height and build. On a normal day, moving him would be near impossible. However, the adrenaline coursing through Naomi is enough to power a locomotive. She shoves her hands under his armpits, anchors her elbows to her sides, and heaves. His feet drag through old dusty rocks.

It's hardest to get his top half up and into the trunk. His legs follow more easily, and she slams the trunk above him. Once inside the sedan, Naomi pauses just long to take a few big gulps of air. In the passenger seat beside her rests her father's briefcase. She tosses it into the trunk on top of her brother before getting into the front to turn the car around and reverse out of the lot.

There'll be plenty to burn tonight.

Fire is the first method she thinks of for how this whole ordeal might end. *It's supposed to be purifying.* People don't think much about controlled burns. *People won't think much about a drunk reverend that sets his own church on fire. It's embarrassing for the town. But teeth survive, don't they? Shit*, she thinks. *Does blood? Do bones?* She can't look anything up to check. Even though eyes are mostly off of her in regard to her Grandma Joyce's death, it will be hard to overlook another dead or missing family member.

At each corner, she waits for an extra beat before turning so the journey is extra rough for her passenger in the trunk.

For twelve years, she waited by herself for her brother to come to her. After Erica died, she coped by imagining what it would be like. She would hear a knock at the door, soft and scared. Through the open curtains, she would see his dark curly head. Tears would fill his eyes — real ones — and they would hold each other, and she would tell him how proud she was that he left. That he chose to protect himself. She would tell him how much she loved him and how she never lost hope. And he would thank her. They would move quickly. Her private studio in Kansas City would become a two-bedroom for a few years. One day, he would tell her he met someone. Someone kind and gentle. Another day, he would pack his things and they would embrace again, and he would move on. *And it would be alright because he left that fucking house and that fucking man.*

"Naomi," a sing-song voice calls from the back.

But that dream won't happen. She can't let him find any more kind and gentle people. He's not her brother. Even though he can't use his eyes anymore, she doesn't know what else he can do — what else the haint can do. She had seen firsthand, for so many years, the damage her father caused. And now Aaron. He abetted Ethan in at least one recent rape. With how casually she heard them speak, likely there were more crimes.

"Naoooooomiii," he calls. She takes the next corner especially sharp and hears him hit the side hard. Then the house comes into view and—

Clara's bicycle.

No, no, no, no. Please no, Naomi begs. She slows the car to give herself even just a few more moments to think. Clara is outside. She's perched on the front steps and her posture straightens when she sees the unfamiliar car. She stands quickly and rushes to her bike. Naomi whips Aaron's sedan into the gravel lot and they lock eyes. Clara sprints to the driver's side.

"Naomi, there's something I have to tell you. Something's happened. I—" She is out of breath and her words rush around a toothpick. "You gotta listen to me. Ethan, he—" Her small hands latch onto the top of the door after Naomi opens it. Naomi's rougher hands grab Clara's and hold them as she shuts the door with her foot.

"Clara, I want to — and I will — but please we can't right now. I can't—" She tries to usher Clara away from the car.

"No, no, no we have to talk now. It's not safe. I think he's coming here. I'm so sorry. I don't want him to hurt you, but Naomi, that thing, I think it's got him—"

"Naooooomiiii," the bastard sings from the trunk.

Clara freezes. The sliver of wood slips from between her down-turned lips and tumbles to the gravel. She looks at Naomi in horror. "No."

"Clara, please—"

"Naoooooooooomiiiiiii."

Naomi turns and kicks the car with every word: "Shut. The. Fuck. UP!"

Clara flinches with each kick and creeps further away. "Is that your brother?" She whispers.

"Yes — no. It—" Naomi pauses and thinks about what Clara just said. "Clara, what did you mean? What's wrong with Ethan?"

"Naomi, is Aaron in the trunk?"

"Clara, please. Something is wrong with Aaron, too. I need to know what you saw with Ethan." Naomi begs but doesn't step closer to her friend.

"His eyes. His eyes, they—" Clara's own eyes begin to unfocus. She's lost somewhere. "Like that day at the river in the lightning bugs. They started to glow green." *She did see the haint.*

"I've seen it, too. In the bugs, in the woods, *under* the fucking river. It's not just you. There's something here." Naomi finally steps forward, and Clara doesn't step back anymore, and Naomi can breathe for the first time in hours. She isn't losing her mind, and neither is Clara. As they have for so many months, they find solace in one another.

Clara takes another step and snags Naomi's hands in her own, sweat slick between them. "Naomi, I'm scared."

Her lovely eyes begin to cry and her nose scrunches and Naomi loves her so much. She tugs her close and they stand breast to breast as their hearts beat so hard against one another that if one gave out the other would start it back up again. Clara curls her fingers like vices around the straps of Naomi's top. Naomi's own weave into her hair. The two women stand together like branches that have grown the entirety of their lives beside each other. When one bends the other curves. The synchronicity that comes to them so naturally.

"It's okay," Naomi whispers. "It's okay. We'll make a plan. I—" For the first time since the initial decision to attack Aaron, Naomi realizes what the endgame of her violent decision will be. *Fire's only for disposing of a corpse. I still need to kill him first.* "We'll take care of it."

Clara finally retreats from Naomi; her hands holding fast to her companion's shoulders. "I'll help. Whatever we have to do, we'll have to do it twice."

Chapter Twenty-Four

Every deer season for the last eight years, Naomi has sat in the blind built in the woods behind Grandma Dottie's house with her rifle in her lap, waiting for a buck. In all of her years of hunting, she found pride in the steadiness of her hand. In how easy it was to pull the trigger when you had a damn good reason to do it. Steady hands are a gift Naomi isn't sure if she was born with or developed. She didn't hunt until she lived alone.

It started as a way to avoid town, to know where her meat came from. Butchering the animals was hard work, but it felt honest, reliable. As long as she owned her rifle, a thick coat, and the land she stood on, she could get deer, turkey, raccoon, and whatever else stumbled through.

But now she looks at her hands, they hurt. They shake like she's in alcohol withdrawal. Her brother's blood is caked under her nails. *I have to remember to take care of that*, she thinks. She's facing a laundry list of blood to clean, evidence to erase.

Clara stands at the front door. Her eyes never leave the driveway. She didn't tell Ethan anything before she left on her bicycle. She tells Naomi that the missing bike alone will be reason enough for him to come after her. It's been a forbidden activity for months now.

Once they settle in Naomi's living room, Clara tells her that Ethan has been locking her in the house, and Naomi matches her confession. She tells her what she learned from the letters of Grandma Dottie's that she didn't show Clara. Finally, Naomi tells her that she heard Aaron and Ethan discussing that he tampered with her birth control. Clara begins to cry and Naomi regrets saying anything.

Even hard truths can be kind though, and she remembers her promise: *Don't be mean, don't be a liar, but don't be a bullshitter.* Naomi says that when Aaron said it, his eyes turned green and that's how she knew he was gone. That's how she knew something had to be done. Clara holds her belly and her shoulders sag. "What if the green bean is evil, too?"

That makes Naomi pause. She was hurt when Clara told her she was pregnant. It was a selfish desire, she knows. She has no place in Clara and Ethan's relationship. She has no right to offer an opinion. But, it stopped feeling like Ethan's child long ago, and only Clara's. Naomi knows — especially now, as they both plan how to escape the cruel men hellbent on destroying their lives — that Clara won't allow Ethan to hurt the baby like he hurt Clara or like Naomi's father hurt her.

And, maybe, Naomi can be a part of the baby's life, if Clara would like. Her daydreams have been overtaken in the past months by colorful tales of teaching a small child to fish and watching Clara breastfeed. The intimacy of a family is so real and so close. Naomi knows what evil is like now. She has always known the earthly version.

She approaches Clara by the door. Sore fingers nearly touch Clara's belly before stopping to look at her friend for approval. Clara nods and Naomi's hands splay across the top of her rounded stomach.

Naomi has no biological relation to this child. There's no expectation of love or devotion that she has to deliver to them. Yet, she longs with every fiber of her being to give them what she always wanted from her own parents. "No. I don't think they'll be born like that. They'll be okay."

Naomi takes a deep breath. She will be there for this baby and Clara in whatever capacity they allow. Be it a friend, lover, wife, or mother. And she will do right by them both. Soft finger pads caress Naomi's cheek and her eyes flutter shut.

"We have to purify them with fire," Naomi whispers, drawing herself back to the problem at hand.

"Why fire? It seems... cruel." Clara holds Naomi's face in her loving palms.

"'But he himself will be saved, yet so as through fire.'" Naomi recalls. "Corinthians."

Clara retracts her hand and Naomi wishes to take it back. "Isn't there any other way?"

"I don't even know if that'll work. What has God ever done for me to make me believe in any of that shit?" Naomi stops touching Clara's belly.

"Couldn't we just take them to the river? Like they do for baptisms. That's purifying. And less hell-fire-y." She doesn't meet Naomi's eye.

Clara is right. Not only is purification by water kinder, but it's also what Great-Grandpa Walter said John did when Kenneth Weir was possessed. There's no explanation for how it worked. He washed him down the river and the haint vanished. *That* haint vanished.

And then they hear it. The rumble of tires on gravel down the drive.

"Oh fuck, we gotta get Aaron out—" Naomi reaches to unlock the front door, but Clara's hand grabs hers in a rush.

"No, no, please no. There's no time. Don't go out there with him. Please," Clara begs. Her eyes fill with tears, and she's right. Ethan nearly spins out in the driveway, leaving a thick plume of dust in his wake. "We gotta block the door. Help me!" Clara runs to the couch and begins pushing as hard as she can. Naomi joins.

They manage to turn it on its side and prop it against the door and even in front of the window. Clara sprints to the kitchen and comes back with chairs. She crams one under the front door handle and another under the handle at the back.

Naomi hauls the small kitchen table in front of the other front window and covers it completely. There is little left to work with inside the ready-to-sell house.

"Get a weapon. Somethin' sharp. We have to get their eyes," Naomi tells Clara. Clara wields a steak knife from the kitchen. Naomi grabs the rifle from the floor. The two watch Ethan pace in front of the house through the small glass windows at the top of the door.

"Baby, I know you're in there. Your bike's out here," Ethan yells. "You know that thing is dangerous in your condition. I'm worried about you, baby," he coos. He paces back and forth a few more times before he stops by Aaron's car. He slowly turns to the trunk.

Fuck me, Naomi chastises herself for not getting Aaron out earlier.

Ethan first goes to the cab of the car and flips the lever to open the back. He walks around to open the trunk. He withdraws a pocketknife and makes quick work of the twine that binds Aaron's arms and legs and throat. He rips the sack off of his head. Ethan stares at him for a moment and Naomi can see the fury burn in his eyes. Even without the supernatural green glow, they still give away the evil within him.

Then Aaron turns and the gaping holes where his eyes once were causes Clara to gasp and drop to the ground. She begins to hyperventilate and Naomi crouches to her level. Her hands hold Clara's face.

"I know, I know—" Naomi repeats. "I'm so sorry. I had to," she pleads.

"If they can't look us in the eye, we can keep fighting. I know. It's just a lot." Clara squeezes her eyes shut for a moment, then pries them open to see Naomi. "I'm really scared, Naomi."

"Me, too," she murmurs.

"I love you." Clara beckons like a lighthouse in a storm.

Of course, she's the brave one to say it, Naomi thinks.

"I love you so much," Naomi responds. "But please tell me again later. When things are okay." She leans in and kisses her forehead before standing.

Ethan's rifling through the backseat of the sedan. Aaron doesn't move. His empty stare is directed at the front door, as if he knows Naomi and Clara are on the other side. Naomi grips the gun tightly in her hands. Extra ammunition is heavy in her jeans' pockets. Ethan returns to Aaron's side with long strips of twine that he hands to her brother. There's a heavy-looking flashlight in his own hand.

"Baby, look at what Naomi did to Aaron — to her own family. You think she won't do that to you too? Baby, I'm real scared." His accent reeks of burnt plastic falsity. It's less authentic than it's ever been.

"I hate him," Clara seethes. "I hate you!" She screams it and Ethan's head whips to the front door. He was speaking to lure her into a response so he could locate them in the house.

"Clara, don't!" Naomi whispers to her.

"Baby, you don't mean that. She's lied to you. She's using your pregnancy hormones against you." Ethan slowly makes his way up the front stairs with Aaron at his heels, grabbing his way up to the porch with his hands.

"You fucked with my birth control you piece of shit! I'm gonna fucking kill you!" Tears spring to Clara's eyes. Her knuckles are white as ghosts around the steak knife.

"I don't even know how that shit works. How could I fuck with it? She's lying to you. Please come out before she hurts you, too," Ethan's voice wavers. It's unnaturally juxtaposed against his facial expression, which is utterly blank.

"You get any closer and I'll do the same fuckin' thing I did to his fuckin' eyes, you scary sack of shit," Naomi joins. "Don't lock eyes with him, Clara," she reminds her.

The two men wander the porch, weapons in hand. Ethan trudges around, knocking on the siding, as Aaron stands at the window by the door. Naomi creeps closer until they stand face to face. His hollow eyes almost seem to look at her. She thinks of her father. *Are his eyes hollow now?* They were soft and fragile. There was so little structure there. She never wanted the two men to be similar.

"This is what you wanted, Naomi," Aaron says.

"I never wanted this. Father wanted you to think we were against each other." Naomi hoists the rifle to her shoulder but, again, her hand quakes. "I wanted you to come here, Aaron. To get away from him."

"You gouged my eyes out, Naomi."

"I had to," Naomi sobs.

"Did Father have to do what he did?" It's a cruel question. It's meant to prod her into doing something stupid. Into getting her into a position to be overpowered, and it nearly works.

"It's not the fucking same." Their inaction will get them killed. Naomi knows it.

She catches Clara's eyes and gestures to the doorknob. Her companion looks perplexed at the thought of opening the door. Naomi places the rifle against her shoulder and nods. The click of the door unlocking doesn't turn Aaron's head.

"You left me in the cellar when we were little. Do you know what I saw down there?" His voice is soft now. It almost sounds honest. Like a child begging for forgiveness. "It wasn't the same for you. I know it wasn't. I was supposed to see God. Speak to Him. I waited 'n waited. I lied to Father. Said that He came to me every time I was down there. Whatever I had to say to get out. Then, one day, He did come to me. I saw what Father saw. The misery and the pain and the love. The love Father gave the only way he could."

Naomi knows that her old house creaks, and when Clara goes to open the door, it'll alert him to their plan.

Naomi kicks the coffee table to cover the squeak as Clara opens the door. His head jerks towards them.

Step by slow step, Aaron inches closer to the doorway.

"But it wasn't when I was a kid in the cellar. He came to me just a few weeks after Father died. This bright, glowing light. Not every day that a man gets to see the light of Heaven. It was as green as the first leaf in spring, and He pried my chest open — my heart open — and climbed inside of me. Now, He and I are one.

"'Then said Jesus unto him, 'Put your sword in its place, for all who take the sword will perish by the sword,'" Aaron murmurs from the open entryway. "One of my favorites," and he smiles. His teeth shine and the bloody pits where his eyes were just an hour ago drip down his face like tears on a church statue.

Without a word, Naomi racks the rifle and Aaron's smile drops at the sound before she loads a round directly into his right leg. It's blown apart, and blood and bits of bone splatter across the white porch before he crashes to the floor.

Naomi chases him out and grabs his collar. She hauls him so that his head hangs over the side of the stairs. Her booted foot is roughly brought down on his nose leaving a crooked bloody mess. She gives a side kick to his reddened cheek so that he faces to the side, and then takes aim again. This time, the blast clears his jaw from his body. It lands in a heap of teeth and blood beneath him.

"Oh my God, she killed him! She killed him, Clara! Please! Run or you're next," Ethan screams to deaf ears. He stands at the end of the porch just ten feet away. His eyes are now spotlights of green aimed at Naomi. The light reflects off the white paint of the house in the low evening light.

Naomi bolts back through the front door. Clara throws herself against it and flips the lock. Naomi shoves her away and towards the closet. She opens it and starts to push Clara inside.

"No, I won't hide," Clara tries to resist Naomi.

"I'll be okay. Come out when it's ready," Naomi says and shuts the door, leaving Clara in a blanket of black.

Naomi rushes to reload the chamber. She grabs the two shells in her back pocket and loads the barrel once more. Heavy metallic sounds echo in the silent house as she racks the gun one last time. Brown eyes remain locked on the front door. She steps closer, watching the windows for a sign of Ethan approaching. With a shaking hand, Naomi unlocks the door and pulls it open ever so slightly.

The eerie shine of Ethan's eyes illuminates the porch. "Where is she?" His voice is no longer fearful or pleading. There's only precise control and loathing. His large hand reaches to push the door open more and Naomi pulls the trigger. Blood explodes over the porch and the doorframe. The force of the blast eviscerates his fingers and hand.

With her last shot disposed of, Naomi tosses the gun on the stairs and runs to the closet. Clara scrambles back to allow her friend some room. Naomi raises her finger to her lips in a silent plea to stay quiet. Naomi shoves Clara further back so she's covered by the clothing. If — *when* — Ethan looks into the closet, he will find Naomi first. She prays that, without telling her companion, Clara will have the good sense to leave when Ethan goes to search the house for her. She's smart. And she has the knife. *She'll be alright.*

Naomi wraps her palm around Clara's and the knife. With quaking fingers, she squeezes tight to let the pregnant woman know that she must keep her only defense close. She must be ready to use it. Naomi reaches up and fiddles through the hanging clothes until she finds a plastic dry-cleaning bag. She rips it off of the hanger and faces the door to wait. Her eye peers through the keyhole.

"Baby," Ethan whines. "Please tell me she hasn't hurt you — hasn't hurt the baby." Ethan's heavy boots are the only sound in the silent house. At this moment, it might even be the whole Ozarks. Not a single cricket chirps outside.

"The baby can't handle stress like this. You could kill it. Do you want to kill my baby?"

Clara holds the knife tight. She places the back of her hand over her mouth. Slowly to ensure her knees won't pop and nothing will be jostled in the closet, Naomi stands upright with the bag in her hands. The screeching of metal scraping against wood is her alert that he has picked up the gun.

Naomi looks through the keyhole again to see Ethan's back turned to her. His remaining hand grips the gun to use as a blunt weapon. Thick fingers tap the barrel impatiently. Ethan's feet stop moving and his head quirks to the side and Naomi knows there is no more time. In a fury, she twists the door handle and throws her weight against the door. As it whips open, she lifts the bag and wraps it over his head. Ethan is knocked off of his feet and the air evacuates her lungs as she collapses on top of him.

Ethan hauls himself up to his elbows and knees. If he gets to his feet, the fight is over. If it comes down to brute strength, Naomi is dead. With all of her might, she tightens the bag around his throat. He sucks in a breath and the plastic suctions over his mouth. She can hear him struggle to breath as he uses his intact hand to try to pull her hand away. Her knee kicks his other hand off of the floor and he falls, hitting his nose to the floor with a sickening crack. Naomi wraps her legs around his waist and flips them over so he can't try to get to his feet again.

Ethan's good hand scrapes at her, trying to claw at her face. Naomi struggles to pull him down lower on her body to keep distance from her eyes. Strong legs constrict around his torso. His hips buck up in an attempt to prevent her from locking him there. In his effort, Naomi tightens the bag over his mouth and throat. Simultaneously, she locks her ankles together, squeezes, and screams.

The door of the closet bursts open. Clara still grasps the knife. Snot bubbles at her nose. "Clara, Clara, please!" Ethan cries. He finally sounds as if he's struggling in their fight. "She's gonna kill me. She's gonna kill me. Please!"

Clara's cries grow louder and erupt through her entire body. She holds the knifepoint down and approaches him. Like a snake, Ethan's hand strikes out and catches her ankle, pulling her to the ground. The knife flies from her hand and scatters across the hardwood floor. Clara lands on her back knocking the wind out of her. Naomi strengthens her grip on the man's windpipe, and he lets go of Clara's leg to try to pry away the bag.

Clara curls in on herself. Her arms wrap around her knees, and she lets out a wail like a banshee calling on her own death. Like she's giving up when Naomi needs her most.

"Don't let her kill me, Clara! Please. Don't let her kill my baby," he pleads. "Not my baby. I want to meet my baby. I'll do good by him, I swear. I'll be better. I'll change, baby."

The burn in Clara's eyes at Ethan's words scorches her face and her misery concedes to fury. She unfurls herself like a spider and crawls across the floor back to the closet. Naomi's strength can't last much longer. Her biceps are close to exhaustion. She needs Clara to do *something*.

"Clara, no, please! I need your help! Please!" Naomi screams. Ethan's desperate attempts to escape become more sporadic. Occasional kicks like spasms. Weak fingers aimlessly smack her arm at his throat rather than pull. His breaths are croaks and chokes. She can't kill him. Not yet. If she does, the haint will rip itself from his chest and find someone else. It won't end. It has to stay locked inside him until they can get rid of it permanently.

With the sturdiness of the doorframe to help her, Clara hauls herself up once more. She reaches into the closet and snatches a metal coat hanger from the closet. The metal untwists in her able hands and the pieces at the top unhook. She bends it until it becomes a thin stake. She straddles Ethan's chest just above Naomi's legs and lifts the coat hanger. His feet scuff the floor and his torso twists slightly in his now lethargic attempts to flee.

Naomi and Clara lock eyes and even before the act, Naomi is filled with relief that she doesn't have to do it herself.

One final time, Clara cries out. It's raw and her voice is fractured and scratched. The coat hanger rips through the delicate tissue of Ethan's right eye. Again and again, the weapon is plunged into his socket. Before she rips it out, she grips the rod with both hands and digs it around in the bloodied hole. Ethan can only open and close his mouth like a fish stranded on dry land. Clara repeats this with his left eye, then slips off of him and crawls away.

Naomi finally releases her boa hold. She grunts as she shoves his limp and sputtering body off of her. Clara and the rifle rest at the foot of the stairs. Her shaking hands hold her belly. The shock is plain on her beautiful face. Specks of blood freckle her fingers and face. Naomi knows then that even with Ethan and Aaron dealt with, their relief will not be immediate.

There will be years of recovery ahead of them both. There will be weeks of sleepless nights with the image of gory sockets and the squishing sound of eyeballs being pulverized. The catfish-like grunts of a man struggling to find his dying breath and the shredded tangles of flesh and teeth left in the aftermath of a gunshot.

Ethan curls on his side and his wailing finally begins with his remaining hand cradling his face. Streams of blood trail through his fingers. "You fucking cunt! You fucking cunts!"

Naomi raises herself from the floor, one hand in Clara's and the other on the barrel of the gun. She drops her companion's hand and raises her tired arms to let loose the final blow, but she pauses. For the second time this evening, she looks to Clara for approval. The woman gives one solid nod. Her chin quivers but her eyes are still a wildfire.

With one last hit of the rifle to his face, Ethan finally shuts up.

Chapter Twenty-Five

The moon glimmers like opal above Naomi and Clara as they load the trunk of the dusty gray sedan with two half-conscious bodies. Ethan doesn't make another sound as they carry him out and to the car. Aaron will never be able to again, although his fingers twitch now and again, which lets them know that he is still alive. Naomi is thankful.

She had the good sense not to remove his head from his shoulders and release the haint, but she didn't consider the blood loss from a wound like he suffered. Clara checks Aaron's pulse, still lightly thumping beneath her fingers despite his bottom jaw being scattered across her front yard. His tongue flops at his throat like a necktie.

Clara rips strips from an old rag and ties it above his knee and one above Ethan's elbow. The bleeding slows to a trickle. A jagged bit of Aaron's tibia and fibula stick out from where his shin is. Fragments of bone intermixed with muscle and skin, and more blood than either woman has ever seen. Clara takes Ethan's jacket off of him and stows it in the car. Naomi collects Aaron's teeth from the front porch and Ethan's from the living room knocked out by the final hit. She tucks them into grocery bags. Separately.

Naomi wonders if the haint helps its host survive wounds like they both suffered. She figures it's best not to waste time. They bind them both in rope by their hands and feet. Although Ethan's eyes are gone, they don't remove the bag from his head. It's hard enough for Clara to see Aaron's eyes. She doesn't need to see her husband like that, too. Especially not after it was her own hands that caused the damage.

Once the men are laying on a tarp in the trunk, Clara wants her and Naomi to both change clothes so they don't leave more evidence in Aaron's car. They quickly wash their hands and arms and change, bagging their bloodied clothes to dispose of later.

The first step is the Kemiwe. It's a sick joke that there's hardly any chance that they'll get pulled over on the way since the lawman of Blaire is tied up in their trunk. They avoid Davis's and instead drive downriver many miles to a dirt road where the Kemiwe is only a few yards from where they park. It's a service route and rarely used.

Naomi drags Ethan out first. She holds him under his arms and hauls him through the sticks and vines. Clara walks behind them with the reloaded rifle on her right shoulder. She looks like a warrior.

When they reach the bank, Naomi drops Ethan and looks at Clara. "Is there anythin' you wanna say?"

"Nope," she responds.

The two men were both stripped naked at the house to avoid any clothes washing ashore. Although catfish are

known for eating just about anything, Naomi has doubts
they have much interest in cotton or denim. Everything her
Great-Grandpa Walter and her Grandma Dottie passed
down has proved to be true thus far. The fear that this
could finally be the part that isn't real burns in Naomi's gut.
If the river doesn't work, they've wasted precious hours that
they need to get away with this. Or at least clear Clara's
name.

Naomi wades into the water and its icy chill makes her
teeth chatter. Clara slides Ethan's body in and her partner
grabs a hold of his shoulders to keep him from floating
away.

Once his entire body is submerged in the river, Ethan's
eyelids burst open, and the strange green light appears like a
distant lighthouse. Clara looks away, but Naomi doesn't. It
grows brighter and brighter. The pinpricks left by the coat
hanger create an opening where the green escapes and
floods into the water where it meets the endless blue of the
river. The viridian begins to fade, and Naomi is overtaken
by a warm wash of water that wraps around her legs and
swirls up and around Ethan's limp and naked body. It
smothers the green pinpricks where his eyes once were.

As quickly as it appears, it washes Ethan away, leaving
nothing left.

Naomi approaches the water one last time with her
brother in tow. She pauses to look at Aaron's deformed
face. She remembers when he was a boy. How he laughed
when she pretended to take his nose. He was so tiny. One
summer, while their father was working and mama was
doing her housekeeping, the siblings stripped to their
knickers and did cannonballs off the rocky ledge of the
Kemiwe.

Naomi waited years for Aaron to seek the same freedom and peace that she wanted. And Naomi sat for those same long years in that same rocking chair on that same porch, and nothing changed. Not her father, her mama, her Grandma Joyce, her brother. Not her either. They all waited like the knick-knacks on Grandma Dottie's shelf, covered in dust and slowly losing color.

Naomi finds herself wondering what she could have done differently. What could she have done to get her brother to understand that he should have left? *Nothing, probably.* Just like she couldn't convince herself in all those years to leave either. Covered in dust on the same shelf. Naomi never really left her place beside them.

Now, all of the Darbys are almost gone. Her mama sleeps soundly at home. Her sister-in-law, too. The three of them are the last Darbys in Blaire. The Curtis family long since passed. Here she stands — ass deep in cold water and soon to be the last blood member of her generation. The weight of every sacrifice, act of cruelty, and tear shed collects on her chest. It is all hers to carry now. It is all hers to fix. There is no progress to be made by older generations. No trauma resolved in her brother or wrongs righted by her mama. The curse is Naomi's alone to lift.

She thinks Clara might stick around while she works through it. But progress has to be made fast. In about four months, the baby will be born. *The only way I can be there for them is if I get my shit together. If I quit standing still.* The next time, it won't be a haint that needs to be destroyed. It will be a human doing the cruel and manipulative things that humans do. It will be a bully at the green bean's school or a man that won't take no for an answer at Clara's work. And those things happen everywhere, whether they stay in Blaire or run off to Kansas City.

Naomi wonders what Blaire will be like with her father, Aaron, and Ethan gone. Will the church stop instructing single moms to marry the cruel men that knock them up? Will there be a new marshal in a few days? What if she stays? Is it her responsibility to help a broken place? Is all the necessary healing even possible in a town whose history is as stained as Blaire's?

If Naomi doesn't try, who else will? No one has yet.

She pulls Aaron's body into the river, and he drops beneath the surface. From his hollow eyes, the same strange green glow emerges and bleeds into the cerulean brilliance of the river. The light illuminates the entirety of his decimated eye sockets and then vanishes like a ghost. And with the light, his body sinks in and disappears until she can neither see him nor feel him.

Naomi swims back to shore where Clara waits with a towel and a gentle hand to pull her out of the cold water and into her warm arms.

Epilogue

The Ozark Channel – May Edition
The Anniversary of the Blaire Baptist Fire

It has been one year today since the catastrophic fire that burnt the Blaire Baptist Church to the ground with the young Reverend Aaron Darby and Marshal Ethan Wilder inside. Rev. Darby left behind his wife, Lily; mother, Margaret; and sister, Naomi. The Darby family has suffered a series of unfortunate luck in past years. First, Rev. David Darby passed from a heart attack; then his mother, Joyce, from a fatal fall; and now Rev. Aaron.

Marshal Wilder is survived by his wife, Clara Wilder, and his son, Jackson, who was born five months after his tragic death. In a community as small as Blaire, every loss is felt tremendously. The Blaire Baptist fire was further complicated by the events leading to the incident. Within Rev. Darby's car were several empty beer bottles, and evidence of hard liquor was found in the remnants of the church along with the partial remains of Darby and Wilder.

The possibility of the fire beginning as an accident, exacerbated by the presence of alcohol was further corroborated by Marshal Wilder's history of alcohol use, which resulted in him being dismissed from his previous position in Jackson County. Investigators ruled the cause of the fire accidental and claim that, along with the alcohol, it was also accelerated due to the presence of an unusually large amount of charcoal and propane collected for the spring barbeque to usher in the new reverend's tenure.

A memorial event is scheduled for this Sunday at the site of the newly built Blaire Baptist Church. There will be a potluck and a sermon. Donations are welcome.

J.W.D. - Journal Entry #1

My mom bought this journal for me a few years back. It took me all that time to figure out what to say. If I had anything to say at all.

I was born in September in Blaire, Missouri. My mom says it was raining on the day I was born and that it washed away her old life. The day I was born, so was she. She says that even though most babies are born crying, that it broke her heart. She wanted me to be born happy, but it doesn't work that way. That you have to try to give happiness to yourself and other people as best you can.

Mom says that the granny woman that helped her during delivery wasn't from here. She says that Blaire hasn't had one in a long time. But we have one now. It's funny, though, calling a young person a granny woman. Mama's only in her early forties but she says that's what she's called no matter her age.

Mama says that I need to be very specific when I'm writing this, because lots of stuff gets lost in time and people that read this in the future might not understand what I'm talking about. So, I'll say it real simple: my mom is the lady that gave birth to me and my mama is the lady that helped her give birth. They didn't get married until I was older and could remember it. That was a few years ago when I was five. I'm eleven now and I'm about to start the sixth grade.

Mom tells me about my dad sometimes, but she's usually pretty sad when she talks about him. I know he died in a fire before I was born. She saved a newspaper clipping about it from a long time ago that I'll keep in this journal. I've seen pictures of him, and Mom says I have his hair and his nose. I asked Mom why she married somebody after Dad, and she said that she fell in love and that Mama helped her during a really hard time when he died and I was born.

But Mom also said that my dad and her didn't get along very well and that that happens sometimes. She said he was mean to her and that she wanted me to have two good parents. She said that she wouldn't have stayed with my dad even if there hadn't been an accident. I didn't use to know that he was mean. Mama said that as we get older, we get to learn more about things. Like how when I was little, I didn't know how to read so they didn't even try to give me big books. But as I got older and better at reading, they started giving me bigger and bigger books.

Mama says that her dad was like my dad, but she doesn't tell me much. Just like everything else, she says that she'll tell me more when I'm older. I feel like I'm old enough to know and I don't like that they keep things from me. They won't tell me things like that, but they tell me kid stories like about hoop snakes which are make-believe monsters that live in the Ozarks. I'm too old to believe in that stuff anymore but Mama says it's important to learn it anyway because it's part of our history.

Tomorrow's my first day of school and I have to go help Mom and Mama with the garden harvest so I can have blackberries in my lunch tomorrow. I don't know how much I'm going to write in this. I don't know what all I have to say or who's going to read this.

Jackson Wilder-Darby

Author's Note

I know that a good deal of this book is likely blasphemous to many people in the area that I love most. While I would much prefer to let the book speak for itself, I fear that people might take this book as a condemnation of their God. It is not. It's a condemnation of anyone using the name of any God to hurt people.

Naomi's journey is one of learning to accept that it wasn't God that hurt her or her brother or so many other people in her town; it was her father, using his God's name to do so. This is the truest evil in religion. Taking a being that should be an incarnation of love and truth, then lying and twisting a good message to gain power or money.

I grew up attending church lock-ins and concerts. I spoke to some friends about their experiences, too. Stories of children being kept up until three or four in the morning with sugar and caffeine and games. Children as young as eleven, exhausted and exhilarated from the excitement of running free and wild around a massive church, being taken into private rooms to be coerced into accepting a God they knew nothing of. Children even being baptized without the consent of their parents.

But I suppose that ain't even the worst of it. In this country, there are also hundreds of years of churches stripping children of their heritage, their culture, their language, their families, and their lives. Hundreds of years of mass burials and unmarked graves. It's heavy. It hurts. We must acknowledge the suffering that Christianity has caused throughout the world and our country in order to hold on to the kind, loving parts and allow justice to flourish.

"He must confess his sin that he committed and must take full reparation, add one-fifth to it, and give it to whomever he wronged" Num. 5:7

Naomi found her God. As I hope many do, even if their God isn't a god at all. Even if it's learning to be gentler with strangers or more patient with your children. Whether it's meditating or gardening or spells or art or church. To each their own.

Acknowledgments

Mara, from the time of this publication, it will be over two years since I last saw you in person and nearly two years since you died. Two years since you knew everything about me. Everything one person could know about another. Except that I never told you what this book was about. I'd drop you off at the doctor, then sit in a McDonald's parking lot writing. When I'd pick you up again, I would tell you that I was writing but not what I was working on. I really fucking regret that now.

It feels like I've lived an entire lifetime since we last spoke. Thank you for everything. I hope that aliens are everything we dreamed they would be.

Everyone who has read this far should check out Mara's art. She is one of the greatest and most sincere illustrators of our generation.

(Mara Padilla / Socials: @marannie or @_girlwithonearm)

Danny, you read this book so many times. You gave me everything I needed to be able to complete it and continue my writing, and there's nothing I can ever do to make the give-and-take in our relationship feel equitable. Thank you for our house and our travels and our pets. Thank you for going to the movies with me and for listening to me talk about them for hours after. Thank you for helping me get back into reading after a decade-long slump.

Thank you for being the kindest, funniest, smartest, tallest, and most beautiful man I've ever met. You're the love of my life.

Kate Martin, Syranda Wiley de Navarro, and Frank Quatrone, thank you for reading this when it was still an ugly larva of a book. Thank you for making me feel good enough to keep going. Kate, to so many more years of writing together. Syranda, to so many more shared meals. Frank, bitch.

Lauren Weiss, thank you for being the final eyes on this. Your review will likely always be the most meaningful.

Peter Kershaw, if you ever see this, I bet you're awful surprised. It's now been six years since I took your film ethics class at SFUAD. I've kept the papers that you edited and the notes you left telling me that I should consider writing. Well, I did it. Thank you for the suggestion.

Kylie Ayn Yockey, I could write off my husband and all of my friends as liars and suck-ups for telling me this book was good enough. It's easy to discredit the kindness of the people closest to you. But I didn't know you very well when I sent you a draft. Your encouragement and direction have made all of the difference. This wouldn't be published without you.

Mom and Dad, thank you for taking me to the Ozarks so much when I was little. It's because of all of our trips and all of the lessons on its history and ecology that I love the area with my entire heart. Dad, thank you to your parents and their parents before them for doing the same. Mom, thank you to you and your mom for instilling a desire for magic in my life.

Thank you to several authors whose books I utilized to learn more about the place I love most in the whole world:

Ozark Folk Magic: Plants, Prayers & Healing by Brandon Weston

A History of the Ozarks, Volume 1: The Old Ozarks by Brooks Blevins

Two Ozark Rivers: The Current and the Jacks Fork with text by Steve Kohler and photography by Oliver Schuchard

Ozark Magic and Folklore by Vance Randolph

Finally, to the Jacks Fork and Current Rivers.